Acting Edition

I0741573

Our Play

by Jessica Moss

ISBN 978-0-573-71140-4

www.concordtheatricals.com
www.concordtheatricals.co.uk

FOR PRODUCTION INQUIRIES

UNITED STATES AND CANADA
info@concordtheatricals.com
1-866-979-0447

UNITED KINGDOM AND EUROPE
licensing@concordtheatricals.co.uk
020-7054-7298

Each title is subject to availability from Concord Theatricals Corp., depending upon country of performance. Please be aware that OUR PLAY may not be licensed by Concord Theatricals Corp. in your territory. Professional and amateur producers should contact the nearest Concord Theatricals Corp. office or licensing partner to verify availability.

This work is published by Samuel French, an imprint of Concord Theatricals Corp.

MUSIC AND THIRD-PARTY MATERIALS USE NOTE

IMPORTANT BILLING AND CREDIT REQUIREMENTS

OUR PLAY premiered at the Wendy Kurka Rust Flexible Theatre at Southeast Missouri State University in Cape Giardeau, Missouri in February, 2024. The production was directed by Kitt Lavoie, with scenic design by Kathy Voecks, properties design by Hannah Bryan, sound design by Cleo Watkins, costume design by Amber Marisa Cook, and lighting and projection design by Christopher George Haug. The production was stage managed by Lyric Stewart. The assistant director was Natalie Williams. The assistant stage manager was Aiden Mueller. The cast was as follows:

BECKY	Peighton Robinson
MARY	Harley Vuocolo
SAM	Oliver Jacquin
WILL	Jake Carpenter
ANTON	Levi Lee
REID	Nicholas Eby
TAYLOR	Josh Neighbors
ALLISON	Evelyn Bunce
SABREENA	Kira Jean-Gilles
DJ	Kennedee Nash
CLAIRE	Brecken Styles
GREG	Drew Post
EMILY	Jodie Lloyd
COOKIE	Jonathan Reynolds

Understudies were Isabel Kissel, Carly Joseph, Em Thomason, Brazos Brooks, Carrington Turner, Tom Drabkin, Reese Simken, Anna Riemenschneider, Deanna Rubach, Lucas Herich, and Ava Barker.

OUR PLAY was developed in June 2023 as part of the Lanford Wilson New American Play Festival and with The Jeanine Larson Dobbins Conservatory of Theatre and Dance at Southeast Missouri State University. The reading was directed by Roxanne Wellington, with assistant direction by Lindsay McLaughlin. Stage directions were read by Josh Neighbors. The cast was as follows:

BECKY . . . . Lizzie White
MARY . . . . Carly Joseph
SAM . . . . Jae Cook
WILL . . . . Jake Carpenter
ANTON . . . . Cameron Cai
REID . . . . .Gabriel Scott Lawrence
TAYLOR . . . . .Noah Hinton
ALLISON . . . . Evelyn Bunce
SABREENA . . . . Natalie Williams
DJ . . . . .Michael Reitano
CLAIRE . . . . .Ava Barker
GREG . . . . Drew Post
EMILY . . . . Lily John
COOKIE . . . . .Zay Williams

Content Warning – school shooting, self-harm and suicide, bullying, drug use.

CHARACTERS

BECKY – She/Her. Real Stage Manager, 16. Organized. Needs a list. Shy and not shy. Someone much happier behind the scenes than onstage. Feels tremendous pressure to succeed. Working on a play for the first time.

MARY – She/Her. Mrs. Gibbs, 16. Character actor who wishes she was an ingénue – in life and onstage. Insecure about appearance. Her dark side scares her, even though most people would not realize she has one. Very ambitious, dreams of being a serious theatrical actor. Extremely sensitive. Allison's best friend? In love for the first time.

SAM – They/Them. Rebecca Gibbs, 16. Non binary. An artist. Makes their own clothes. Some kind of "dark" aesthetic – this could be goth, this could be punk, this could just be that they like horror movies or Edward Gorey's art. Introspective, startlingly wise, confident enough to be still, confident enough to be different, confident enough to be themselves. This confidence is not easy; it was really, really hard won. Also on a championship winning robotics team. Sam was in a traumatic school incident (at another school) in 8th grade.

WILL – He/Him. Dr. Gibbs, 17. Athlete with performance ability. Older brother. A positive thinker. Charmed and charming. A little bit of a golden boy, or at least a golden aura. Elastic and loose-limbed, like a slinky.

ANTON – He/Him. Howie Newsome, 16. Good real-life friend of DJ, but Anton has an online community that he is closer to. Tried out because DJ did. A gamer. Analytical. A follower at this point in his life, and a natural collaborator. Starting to think he could be a leader. You wish you got to do a group project with Anton.

REID – He/Him. Constable Warren, 17. Recently got in trouble for stealing equipment from the school gym. He might be doing the play as a punishment, or at the suggestion/mandate of a guidance counsellor. Impulsive, intimidating, prone to explosion. But he is softer than he lets on.

ALLISON – She/Her. Emily Webb, 16. A class clown who occupies the position of a cool girl: a unicorn. People tend to think she has no problems; she has a feeling that that is a huge reason behind her success and wants to keep them thinking that way. As ambitious as, and constantly in competition with Mary, who is her best friend.

TAYLOR – Any gender, change pronouns as appropriate (this script uses they/them). Stage Manager, 17. Cannot take a compliment (deeply craving compliments). Terrified of failure. Struggles with dissociation: is life real? Am I real? Scared, but deeply craving to reveal a deep silliness, giddiness, anything vulnerable. Self-deprecating.

SABREENA – She/Her. Simon Stimson, 16. Wants to fit in. Intense difficulty with school (recently diagnosed ADHD) but doesn't tell anyone about it. Started the school in the middle of freshman year and feels she never fully caught up to anyone. Deeply loving and in need of a place to put her love. Disorganized, but extremely capable; hyper-focused when she cares about something.

DJ – Any gender, change pronouns as appropriate (this script uses she/her). Mr. Webb, 17. Stoner philosopher. "Yeah, man." Doesn't have to study to make excellent grades. History buff, cinephile, lover of beauty. Desires and prioritizes experience. Learning about the cosmos. Lonelier than they let on.

CLAIRE – She/Her. Mrs. Webb, 17. Emily's best friend since grade four. Very insecure about cystic acne; has tried Accutane and it hasn't worked. On the swim team – has non-stop wet hair, and her acne is aggravated by the chlorine. She regularly hits her cheeks, or licks the backs of her hands and puts them on her cheeks, to try and stop the burning feeling. Emily is trying to stop her from doing this.

GREG – He/Him. George Gibbs, 16. Loud. Appears confident. "How dare you." A vicious and cultivated sense of fashion. Pop culture expert, and has great throwback knowledge for movies, fashion, dances, music of the past (particularly Club Kid culture). Physically not dominant, but dominates every room he's in. Being harassed by hockey players.

EMILY – She/Her. Mrs. Soames, 17. Claire's best friend since grade four. Has multiple honors classes with Allison this year, and they sit together in them. Wants to be a doctor. Extremely studious and grades – focused. Has a 10-year plan, and it requires getting into a top college. Doing the play to boost extracurriculars. From a wealthier family than most of the others. Has cats.

COOKIE – He/Him. Joe Crowell, 17. Bradley Cooke, called Cookie. First play ever. Hockey player. Quiet until he's not. His dad recently passed away from cancer. Has the aura of someone who has lived through a tragedy – but is that just what everyone is putting on him?

Please cast with a mindful and sensitive eye to diversity, and represent the diversity in your community.

SETTING

A high school theatre before, during and after a production.
Present day.

TIME

In the theatre, right now.

AUTHOR'S NOTES

A [/] indicates a point of interruption, where the following line begins.

Dialogue in two columns   or more   is simultaneous!

CAPS DON'T NECESSARILY MEAN YELLING, and ellipses [...] don't necessarily mean a pause. They indicate something's happening in the character's train of thought, but that can manifest in lots of different ways, often to indicate a character thinking, or searching for how to use language. It's fine to take a beat there if that feels right to you, but you don't have to. The play needs to move at pace and can't be bogged down by too many silences, so earn the ones you really need.

Fast. Real fast.

The play should ideally run without an intermission, but if you need one, take it after Act One. You can have Becky yell "Intermission!" while she's trying to calm everyone down.

All the characters in the play should carry a printed script through Act One, in various states of use/disarray. I offer to you that all props other than the script can be mimed, and there might not be much more than chairs, blocks, or maybe a ladder as a set (à la *Our Town*).

The song choice in Act Two should be chosen by the cast/crew of your production as a group. Can be a pop song, a school/choir song, whatever feels right for what this moment is to the characters, and to the play. Something to think about is if it's a moment of counterpoint to the end of Act One, where we see the group having a lot of fun, but being quite chaotic; is this the chance to show how they have come together as an ensemble? If it isn't too stressful for your group, you might want to pick a few songs and have the actor playing Sam choose one spontaneously each performance. If you have legit singers in the group, it's conceivable to me that some of these characters are in choir and love to sing, complete with a few of them trying a harmony. But if you don't have any singers, that's also totally fine...maybe better.˙

THANKS

Special thanks to everyone at the Lanford Wilson New American Play Festival and SEMO, particularly Kitt Lavoie, Roxanne Wellington, and the incredible students; C 'Meaks' Meaker, Rachel Greene, Lindsay Partain, and Keiko Green; Sara Naumann, Kelly Cavanagh, and Josh Neighbors for the rides (Jae Cook for the assist); Rosey Strub and The Wilder Estate; and Marsha, David, Chris, and everyone at Juilliard.

For the real Sabreena
Clever girl...

(House lights are up.)

*(When all the audience is in, and before they quieten, **BECKY** enters.)*

(She has a headset and a clipboard. Stage management gear.)

BECKY THE STAGE MANAGER. Um. OK.

The play's called *Our Town*.

It's *Our Town*.

(She looks at her clipboard.)

By Thornton Wilder.

(She looks up from her clipboard and squints into the audience.)

I'm Becky. Stage Manager. The real one, not in the play. I would *not* be in the play, ha. Not that it's – I – mmm. I don't mean it like that. I'm the stage manager. That's all.

(She looks at the clipboard.)

"Introduce self." Check. *(She crosses it off.)*

I'm not that good at being a Stage Manager, if you're – I'm just organized. I don't actually like being in charge or telling people what to do? Well maybe I – sometimes I like telling people what to do, but – no, I really like telling people what to do, sometimes, and I like spreadsheets. I love spreadsheets. And pens. And I liked when we were rehearsing when we'd all be there together, it felt...

with talking it's like you start doing it and then you remember you don't like doing it in front of people?

OK. "Set up space like SM in *OT*."

This is the theatre. The booth, where I sit is up there.

> *(She points up and behind the audience, or to wherever the actual booth is.)*

This is the house, where the audience sits. You're in the house.

> *(The house lights can start to go down now. So slow as to not be noticeable, if possible.)*

This is the stage.

There are wings. "Backstage." Where we store props and stuff, and where you wait before you go on. Like... here? Here?

If you exit stage right – that's this way, it's the actor's right, I always mess that up – there's a little stairwell. That's like pre-backstage. You wait there before you wait in the wings.

Yeah?

I'm doing like what the Stage Manager does in the – 'cause I thought that would maybe be like... Taylor did it in the play and they were so good, they like –

> *(**BECKY** makes a gesture like how **TAYLOR** played the Stage Manager.)*

> *(She listens. She looks back to the audience.)*

And if you go up the stairs, there's a drama room where classes happen, and we use it to rehearse and keep costumes and props in.

Little room where we do makeup, off the drama room.

Then you go out the doors to a long hallway. That way, there's an entrance to the field. Sometimes those outside doors lock? It's kind of private there so people go out there to like…whatever, but then sometimes they get locked out.

Other way out of the drama room, there's lots of hallways, and eventually you get to the lobby. We'll say it's, I don't know. Here? *(A part of the stage.)*

"Theater." Real but not. Magic and friends. Right?

I don't honestly know why we do this play. It's good, I mean, well, but it's called *Our Town*? I don't live in a town. This play has like. Milkmen? Who have horses? *(She kind of laughs.)* People go and have ice cream sodas? It's not *My Town*.

> *(She looks around the theatre.)*

> *(She takes a step.)*

Today we're doing this scene which is a wedding. Emily's wedding. Emily's big day. That's what we're doing at this rehearsal. So everyone's in it, so everyone's called today.

> *(She scans the theatre.)*

(Does she shiver?) Everyone's supposed to be here. I called everyone. I'm the stage manager, so they have to come because I called them. It's three fifty-nine p.m., and we're doing the first rehearsal with everyone, and everyone's here.

The show's in a month. We're not ready.

> *(She kind of laughs.)*

Some people are, Will and Mary, they're fine, Mary is such a good actor, but there's so much other stuff that is like, nowhere. I don't know what to do about that. I really don't. How do I fix – am I supposed to fix it?

I have no idea how. Ms. Welles tells me stuff but at the center there's this hole like: *but how?* No one teaches you what you actually need, you know? People keep saying "it will be OK," but no one says how. So I find it very hard to believe that it's going to be OK. Or as good as it's supposed to be. It seems impossible and I don't think I can, I don't think I know what to do and I didn't ask for this job, I'm not –

> (**WILL** *and* **MARY** *enter to the stage area.*)

> (**BECKY** *sees this and stops herself – she almost can't believe her own stage magic.*)

BECKY. *Oh.*

That's them. That's Will and Mary. They're here.

MARY. Of course we're here. It's rehearsal.

BECKY. Yeah. OK. Will and Mary play Dr. and Mrs. Gibbs. They're awesome. I never have to worry about them showing up, or knowing their lines, because they always do.

> (**SABREENA** *sits in the house, or on the edge of the stage, with nothing to do. Watching* **WILL** *and* **MARY**.)

Mary has been in the play and the musical every time. She usually plays very serious, supporting parts. We did *The Music Man* and she was the mayor's wife, and she was really funny though. Will broke his leg last year and so his parents didn't want him to play hockey again, so. He's in the play.

MARY. "Now Frank don't be grouchy. Come out and smell the heliotrope in the moonlight."

BECKY. This is like their scene together. They're in their garden.

MARY. Oh God.

*(While they continue, **ANTON** and **DJ** quickly cut across the stage, from backstage towards the lobby, whispering. **DJ** is doing a kind of "excited" dance. They wave at **WILL** and **MARY**, who wave back, without stopping.)*

*(**SABREENA** watches this without being seen.)*

*(**BECKY** sees everything as if for the first time.)*

BECKY. What are they – oh no. DJ, where are you going?

DJ. I am going to the library, Rebecca. To learn things.

BECKY. DJ.

DJ. *(Leaving.)* It'll be OK!

BECKY. Do you want me to give up?

*(**BECKY** doesn't realize, but **DJ** hears this, even though she keeps going.)*

WILL. What?

MARY. I suck.

WILL.	**ANTON**.
No you don't.	*(As he goes out the door.)* You don't suck, Mary.

MARY. That line is hard. It's like very /"gather round children, let me tell you a story of the past."

WILL. "In my day," yeah, exactly!

MARY. "Let me turn on the Victrola and we'll do that modern foxtrot."

WILL. *(Laugh.)* You're so funny. What even is heliotrope?

SABREENA. I was just wondering that!

*(**MARY** looks at **SABREENA**.)*

BECKY. That's Sabreena. I didn't even see her there.

MARY. *(To* **WILL***.)* It's a flower. It's purple. It's supposed to smell good, I looked it up.

> *(Unseen by* **WILL** *and* **MARY***,* **ALLISON***,* **EMILY** *and* **CLAIRE** *enter from backstage.)*

> *(***SABREENA** *kind of waves at them, but if they see her, they don't respond.)*

WILL. Damn! That's my favorite line in the play now, calling it. I wanna do that. I wanna smell the heliotrope in the moonlight. I'm gonna be like –

> *(He pretends to be Dr. Gibbs jumping off the porch, and actively smelling heliotrope.)*

> *(He picks some pretend heliotrope and gives it to her.)*

> *(They link arms and start to walk like they do in the play.)*

Maybe I should do one of these –

> *(He spins her. Then he does that thing where you jump and click your heels in mid-air.)*

> *(He gets down on one knee and opens his arms to* **MARY***.)*

MARY. I'm too heavy.

WILL. No you're not.

> *(She sits on his knee.)*

EMILY.
THAT'S SO CUTE.

CLAIRE.
Aww, you guys look so sweet like that!

ALLISON. Shhh!

> (**MARY** *leaps off.*)

BECKY. That's Allison. Emily, and Claire, and Allison. Emily and Claire are best friends, and Allison plays Emily. In the play. There's play Emily and real Emily. We didn't really talk but she's really nice and everyone likes her. I like her. I don't know her, but I really like Allison.

Keep going, please!

ALLISON. (*A thing they do.*) Mary, my angel, from heaven!

MARY. Allison, light of my life!

> (*They head off towards the lobby.* **CLAIRE** *is patting her cheeks.* **EMILY** *sees this and takes her hands.*)

EMILY. Stop.

CLAIRE. No, it hoits.

EMILY. Stop.

ALLISON. It'll be OK, Becky.

BECKY. Hngggg.

ALLISON. I know. But it will! I mean, it'll be what it is. It'll –

BECKY. Go on.

> (**ALLISON** *nods.*)

> (*They share something – a shrug? An almost smile?*)

> (**ALLISON** *runs off.*)

> (**WILL** *looks at* **MARY**, *smiling.*)

WILL. What is that?

MARY. Oh, it's just this thing we do, I don't know.

WILL. Cool. (**WILL** *drops to a knee.*) No, wait.

> (*He does his heel clicky thing, his gathering the heliotrope thing, this time even bigger, and then drops to a knee and holds out his arms to* **MARY**.)

> (**MARY** *looks at him.*)

Everyone's gone, don't worry.

MARY. You can't do that in the play. We're the old people.

WILL. We're the parents! We're in charge! Get over here.

> (**MARY** *sits on his knee.*)

> (**MARY** *puts her arm around his shoulders.*)

Yeahhhhh!

MARY. I'm always old in the play. /I never get to –

WILL. Who did you want to be? Emily?

MARY. (*Yes.*) No. I don't know. I guess there isn't really a part for me in this play. I don't know if there's a part for me in any play.

WILL. But you're /in the play. You're always in the play.

MARY. It's. /Difficult to explain. But I –

REID. (*Offstage, from lobby.*) I'M NOT YELLING, I WASN'T YELLING, I DON'T NEED TO CHILL, EVERYONE IS ALWAYS TELLING ME NOT TO YELL WHEN I'M NOT YELLING. GOD, I'LL –

SABREENA.	(**REID** *opens the door*
What's that about?	*to the theatre from*
	the lobby and looks
	in –)

REID. There's people there, there's... *(He closes the door and goes, but they hear:)* ARGH.

> *(WTF?????)*

SABREENA. Whoa. Somebody check the equipment room again.

COOKIE. Hey.

> (**COOKIE** *pokes his head on from backstage.)*

> (**MARY** *quickly stands up off* **WILL**'s *knee again.)*

MARY.	**WILL**.	**SABREENA**.
(So nice.)	*(So nice.)*	*(So nice.)*
Hey Cookie, how are you?	Hey man.	Heyyyyy...

COOKIE. Oh. Sorry.

MARY.	**WILL**.	**SABREENA**.
It's OK.	No, no worries.	How are you doing?

COOKIE. Have any of you seen my script?

SABREENA. What does it look like?

COOKIE. Like a script.

> *(They all start to look for it.)*

MARY.	**SABREENA**.
Does it have your name on it?	Does it have your – yeah.

COOKIE. *(I'm an idiot.)* No.

MARY. Are your lines highlighted?

COOKIE. Uh. No. There's some writing in it though. Like a list on one of the back pages?

Dammit. K, if you find an extra script, it's mine.

SABREENA.	WILL.	MARY.
I'll keep an eye out.	Sure man.	OK.

(**COOKIE** *goes off the way he came.*)

MARY. Should we have said something? About how sorry we are, or –

WILL. I've said that like four times, I said it at the funeral. I try to be nice to him, but I don't know /what to say.

SABREENA.	MARY.
I feel so bad.	No you are, that was nice.
One day you just don't have a dad anymore. And Cookie seems normal.	

MARY. Can you – I'm sorry – but can you. I feel weird doing the scene and being watched. Just do you mind, while we're rehearsing?

SABREENA. You know it's a play, right? Like. People will eventually be watching.

MARY. I know, but there's been a lot of activity, and just/ while we're rehearsing if you could...

SABREENA. OK. Yeah. OK. (*She exits towards the lobby.*)

MARY. From, uh...?

(**WILL** *offers her his arm.*)

(*They link arms and start walking.*)

WILL. You know the best part?

MARY. (*...*) Oh my god, I thought we were starting and I was like, /"when does he say that?" and I was freaking out, what.

WILL. Oh, ha ha, no. When you're not onstage but someone says your character's name? I love when that happens. /It's like you're –

MARY. Oh yeah! I also love – sorry, I interrupted.

WILL. It's OK, what?

MARY. No, what were you /gonna say.

WILL. Just like. They say your name and it's like you're there. Even if you're not? I feel that I get pulled into the play even though I'm backstage or something. You're there even though you're not. What were you gonna say?

MARY. Oh, it was *not* that smart, /forget it.

WILL. Come on, what is it.

MARY. No, it's just my stupid little brain –

WILL. Come on. Tell me?

MARY. I like when I'm dead. Our scenes are my favorite though.

WILL. Me too. Getting to act with you is like. It's so money. "Come out and smell the /heliotrope in the moonlight!"

MARY. That's my line, I don't sound like that! "Come out and smell the heliotrope in the moonlight!"

WILL. Do you – OK, I'm just gonna ask you something. 'Cause like. We can just talk, right?

Is Allison going to the homecoming dance with anyone? Do you know?

> (**MARY** *looks at him.*)

Don't tell, OK? I just wanted to ask because we're friends.

MARY. Um. I don't know.

WILL. And you're friends.

MARY. Not really.

WILL. You have a thing.

MARY. No, I don't really, we don't really, we're not like super close or anything, that's just some – I don't know.

WILL. I thought you were really tight. Do you know if she has a boyfriend?

(*Beat.*)

MARY. She probably does. I heard her talk once about going out with this friend of her brother's and they went to some old playground and he was boring so she did cartwheels.

WILL. Huh.

MARY. I've heard her talk about lots of guys like that. She used to date some guy who was like training for the Olympics in skiing.

WILL. Right. Cool.

MARY. I mean I don't know, but –

WILL. Yeah, no. It's not a big deal, I was talking to some other guys and they said we should all just pair off and get everyone a date so that everyone in the play goes together. So it doesn't really matter, but I was wondering.

MARY. Who would I go with?

WILL. I don't know, we'll all just go together.

MARY. But I'd be /paired with someone.

WILL. Some people want to ask other people so after we know that then we'll see who is left over.

MARY. Oh.

WILL. You'll come, right? It won't be fun if you don't come.

MARY. Depends who asks me, I guess.

WILL. Someone really fun. I'll make sure – come on, I'm going to make sure you get the best date. Gotta take care of my wife! So just think about it. Yeah?

You want to start from the beginning?

MARY. Actually. Uh. I don't think that playground guy is her boyfriend. I don't know. I don't know if she has a boyfriend or not. So.

WILL. Oh. OK. *(He makes like a victory gesture.)* Whoo, I'm in! Ha ha.

MARY. *(She goes off towards the lobby.)* Mm. Yeah. Actually, I need to pee, so hold on.

BECKY. Those two take it seriously. They're going to be fine. Um. That yelling thing? I remember that, I forgot but I remember but I never...can we go back a bit and go to the lobby now? I mean. Let's go to the lobby. Just a few minutes ago. Ha. See what I said about not being like super good? Yes. I'll. Take you to the lobby. Or the lobby will come here.

> *(While **BECKY** says this, **TAYLOR**, **SAM**, and **REID** enter.)*
>
> *(**TAYLOR** sits, with their script, away from **SAM**.)*
>
> *(**SAM** sets up a painting area: canvas, paints, brushes...)*
>
> *(**REID** watches **SAM** over their shoulder.)*
>
> *(**SAM** is aware but tries to keep painting for a bit.)*

Yeah! *Okayyyyy*! Out in the lobby, Sam is setting up. They're gonna make some posters for the show. Sam takes art, not drama, and music. They're really artistic. Like actually.

That's Reid. He's the one you saw just now. Reid is um. I don't really know Reid. He plays the policeman in the town. And then he's dead, at the end.

Oh, and there's Taylor, the stage manager. The "me." Taylor spends every rehearsal learning lines. 'Cause being the stage manager is really, really stressful and nobody sees that you just work and worry all the time.

SAM. Can I /help you?

REID. Sorry, just. Wanted to see.

> (**DJ** *and* **ANTON** *walk through, heading towards outside.)*

SAM. It isn't anything yet, so you won't have anything to look at.

REID. That's OK. I'll see it be born. Do you know what it's going to look like?

Look, I'll turn away, so I won't watch you.

> *(He turns his back to* **SAM**.*)*

SAM. You don't have to do that.

REID. No, it's good, I don't want to get in the way of an artist at work y'know.

SAM. I want it to be – this might sound kind of cute, but it shouldn't be cute. That's not what I intend. I want it to be the colors that leaves turn in the fall. And like. Those days when the trees are all of those fall colors and the leaves are falling all around, like they're almost like rain –

REID. And they shimmer? Like little yellow leaf tornados all around you.

SAM. Yeah! And the sky is like really blue.

REID. Those days are the best.

SAM. Yeah.

REID. *(Sneaking a look at **SAM**.)* Cool. Does it bother you? Being Rebecca?

SAM. Why?

REID. I don't know. 'Cause it's a small part. And it's a girl part. And you're...

> *(**SAM** looks at **REID**. **REID** turns away.)*

SAM. What am I?

REID. Uh. Well. You know. You're –

> *(**EMILY**, **CLAIRE**, and **ALLISON** come out of the theatre.)*

SAM.	**EMILY**.	**CLAIRE**.
Are you trying to find out, or are you trying to tell me?	You just need to stop touching it – no it's not, you're the only one who notices.	It's like especially disgusting today, of course it would be.

REID.
Whoa.

*(They see what's going on with **SAM** and **REID**.)*

SAM. What do you want to say? What do you want to know?

REID.	**CLAIRE**.
Relax –	Sam, are you OK?

SAM.	**EMILY**.
I don't need to be relaxed. I'm fine.	What's going on?

REID. But you don't need to be, like –

SAM.	CLAIRE.	EMILY.
What?	Reid, chill.	Don't yell at
/What am I?		Sam.

REID. Aggressive, whoa, I'M NOT YELLING, I WASN'T YELLING, I DON'T NEED TO CHILL, EVERYONE IS ALWAYS TELLING ME NOT TO YELL WHEN I'M NOT YELLING. GOD, I'LL GO, THEN –

(He opens the door to the theatre and looks in –)

There's people there, there's... *(He closes the door.)* ARGH.

BECKY. What's going on? I heard yelling. You're supposed to be rehearsing.

TAYLOR.	ALLISON.	SAM.
I AMMMMM.	We are, we're going to.	I'm doing the banner.

*(**ALLISON**, **CLAIRE**, and **EMILY** go towards the makeup room.)*

CLAIRE. Sam, do you want to come with us?

*(**SAM** looks at **REID**. **REID** rolls his eyes.)*

SAM. Nope, I'm OK. I want to figure this out.

CLAIRE & EMILY. OK.

*(**ALLISON**, **CLAIRE**, and **EMILY** go off.)*

*(In real life, in the past, **BECKY** would go back to the theatre. But she stays to watch the rest.)*

*(**SAM** goes to the canvas. **REID** watches **SAM**.)*

REID. Hey. Hey, look, I wasn't trying –

*(**SABREENA** comes out of the theatre.)*

REID.	SABREENA.
(Continued.)	Hey!
To be an assh –	
GODDAMMIT.	

> (**SABREENA** *is stopped in her tracks by* **REID***'s voice.*)

REID. Not you, sorry, /I didn't mean, that wasn't for you, I –

SABREENA. No, don't worry about it. I get it.

> (**SABREENA** *goes off the same way that* **DJ** *and* **ANTON** *did.*)

REID. Is that everyone? Have I pissed off every single girl in this play yet? Not that – ugh, God damn.

Sam, I didn't want that to happen, I just, sometimes there's a flash and I do something.

I like that color. *(He points.)* It's like October.

SAM. What I'm going for.

REID. Best month. All the other months wish they were October.

SAM. Not June. June is happy being June.

REID. June's my favorite month.

SAM. I thought October was /your –

REID. Season. Fall's my favorite season. June's my favorite month. And my favorite flower is the hyacinth.

SAM. Mm. I like being Rebecca. To answer your question. She's funny.

REID. She is /funny. And smart.

SAM. And she's like a brat – yeah. But in a bratty way. They said I'm going to wear like a little dress. So. Make it *fashion*. Next year, if I was going to do it, I would do costumes.

Do you like being... /Who are you playing again, oh yeah.

REID. Constable Warren, I mean, not really, but sure? And some random dead guy? I like that one. 'Cause I'm dead.

SAM. Right.

REID. No, really. I was murdered. They slit my jugular and severed my limbs and I bled out on the floor. The only people who can see me are the ones who are capable of similar deeds.

> (**SAM** *doesn't know what to say to that. So they paint.*)

Hey. Hey.

SAM. I'm trying to /work.

REID. I was kidding, I thought that –

SAM. What do you expect me to say to something like that?

REID. Hyeah, I, sorry –

SAM. I'm trying to work. It might not look like work, but that's what I'm doing.

REID. I'm sorry, I didn't mean to – I don't mean to do this stuff.

SAM. I don't care what you mean or you don't mean, don't do it.

REID. Yeah. Yeah. You heard about me and the equipment room?

SAM. That's not what this is about, /I don't know all the information about that, but don't talk to me like that.

REID. I know, I know. But you know?

SAM. I heard something.

REID. I don't even know why I did that. Same thing, like the flash? Just some crazy, hot feeling, and it happens, and I don't, like, I'm trying, in my head I'm saying, "don't blow up," but then it happens and I do it. And then it's too late. And like. I'm not this guy that everyone seems to think I am. But then I act like that. I blow up. I scream at whatsername there. So maybe I am. But I'm not, but – and I don't know how to stop it. What did you say? I don't like explaining my stuff because people don't understand it, that's exactly how I feel, all the time.

> *(While* **REID** *speaks,* **GREG** *enters from the hallway. He throws down a script at* **TAYLOR***'s feet but walks past. If* **REID** *has gotten closer to* **SAM***, that sends him back.)*

TAYLOR. Are you ready?

GREG. I have to go to the bathroom.

TAYLOR.	**SAM**.
Greg, please –	Sabreena.

GREG. DO YOU WANT ME TO GET TOXIC SHOCK SYNDROME?

TAYLOR. Oh my god, you're –

GREG. *(Going back towards the bathroom.)* HOLDING IN YOUR PEE GIVES YOU KIDNEY STONES. *(He's gone.)*

> *(***TAYLOR***,* **SAM***, and* **REID** *look at each other.)*

TAYLOR. He's fine.

GREG. *(Off-stage.)* WE DON'T TALK ENOUGH ABOUT URINARY HEALTH, TAYLOR.

SAM.   Maybe you should talk to Greg about anger management, /he seems to have it figured out.

TAYLOR.   Oh, yeah, he's a Zen master.

> *(Do they all kind of laugh? Does* **BECKY** *kind of, too?)*

REID.   Hyeah. No. They made me go talk to that bird lady a while ago.

SAM.   ...Bird /lady?

TAYLOR.   I know exactly who you're talking about.

REID.   The one who said I should do the play, that it would help me "integrate," the guidance woman who /looks like an ostrich.

TAYLOR.   Ms. Mustard.

SAM.   ...That's not /her name.

TAYLOR.   I assure you that it is.

REID.   You know, she's got those big round glasses, and her neck is /so long.

SAM.   Her neck is sooo long. And her name is Ms. Mustard?

TAYLOR.   In the guidance room. With a candlestick. It's definitely her name, I had to see her when Madame Schreiber thought I was putting too much pressure on myself after I cried during a grammar quiz. It wasn't about the quiz, it was about the northern white rhinoceros. She used the word "integrate?"

REID.   Yeah.

SAM.   I saw the other one. Miss Cooper. /Who also looks like a bird, kind of, but not –

REID.   You did?

TAYLOR.   More like an owl.

SAM.   Yessssssss.

*(**SAM** and **TAYLOR** make owl faces that are
also the face of poor Miss Cooper.)*

(Doing Miss Cooper.) "Sam, ooh, we are with you and
support you on your journey, ooh. Be whoo you want
to be, ooh."

REID. Yeah. Like that's easy.

TAYLOR. It's easy for Greg.

(They laugh.)

SAM. No, of course it's not easy. Not to figure it out and
then not to get up every day and actually be that person.
Instead of just playing the part that everyone assumes
you are. Or wants you to be. Or who you were, at one
point, so you're supposed to be that person forever even
though you can't anymore. Those guidance ladies are
nice but they don't –

*(At some point, **SAM** has moved around the
canvas, but left their water cup on the other
side.)*

(They look for it, reach to get it –)

*(**REID** has grabbed it and holds it out
to them.)*

Thanks. What was I saying?

REID.
The part that everyone
assumes you are.

TAYLOR.
The...

*(As **SAM** moves around the canvas, **REID**
follows, holding the cup for them.)*

*(**TAYLOR** realizes they are watching the
beginning of something.)*

SAM. That sounds cornier than /I mean it to.

REID. No, no, I, yeah.

> (**MARY** *comes out of the theatre, visibly upset.*
> *She beelines through towards the hallway.*)

> (**SAM** *dips a brush in the cup* **REID**'s *holding*
> *for them.*)

You know those days we were talking about earlier?
That you're trying to paint? Those are the days I see
my brother. He died but. Sometimes I can still see him.

I really am sorry. For saying that stuff earlier.

SAM. I didn't want to hear about someone cutting out
anyone's organs, even though I have a, you know.
Penchant for the macabre. Even though I like weird
stuff.

REID. Right. I'm sorry, I –

SAM. 'Cause. You know I've seen a dead body. A few. /And.

REID. Yeah.

SAM. *(Continued.)* I've seen a ghost too. I do see them.

REID. Really? Was it... /one of the –

SAM. No. Not the one I'm thinking about. It was an old
lady. I saw her on a train.

> *(They look at each other.)*

BECKY. Hey, Sam? Sorry to interrupt.

SAM.	**REID**.
It's OK.	You're not interrupt...ing.

BECKY. What do you think this play's about?

SAM. I think it's about people. These specific people. And
what happens to them.

BECKY. Yeah. What do you mean?

SAM. I mean they live and they die. Which happens to everyone. But they also are like… I mean it's like 1900 and their lives don't look like – /like no one has a phone.

REID.	**BECKY**.
Yeah, it's…	They don't look like us.

SAM. *(Continued.)* And they talk – yeah. The first few times I read it I was like "what is this."

REID.	**TAYLOR**.
Me too!	Totally.

SAM. Right?

REID. The first time I fell asleep.

SAM. I did too!

> *(**REID** holds his hand up for a high five, which **SAM** does not see. They continue.)*

But that's kind of the point of it. How you can still be in a town with people, or you can watch a play with people that aren't you, and it can still be about you. *(To **REID**.)* Any ideas?

REID. Oh, I don't know.

BECKY. That's OK.

REID. I mean, it's about Emily. She's the lead. I mean, the stage manager's the lead, I guess in terms of lines, /but it's really like…

TAYLOR. Thank you.

REID. *(Continued.)* It's about how she grows up. She grows up in the world, the, the town because she falls in love and she gets married and then she grows up because she's dead and then she grows up because she realizes what she used to have and what being alive is. But she only realizes it when she can't have it anymore.

SAM. Yeah. That's it. That's what it's actually about.

BECKY. Thanks, Sam. Thanks, Reid.

> (**REID** *helps* **SAM** *clean up and go.*)
>
> (*He offers them a hand to stand up.*)
>
> (**SAM** *notices. Takes his hand.*)
>
> (**GREG** *has returned to* **TAYLOR.**)
>
> (*He opens and flips through the script.*)
>
> (**TAYLOR** *inhales, about to start.*)

GREG. Wait.

TAYLOR. Oh my /God.

GREG. THIS ISN'T MY SCRIPT.

TAYLOR. Whose /script is it?

GREG. I don't know.

TAYLOR. Where's /your script?

GREG. I don't know, Tay-lorrrrr. But we have to solve the mystery!

TAYLOR. No we don't, you can use mine.

GREG. YOU NEVER LET ME SOLVE MYSTERIES. HOW IS OUR DETECTIVE AGENCY EVER GOING TO GET OFF THE /GROUND?

TAYLOR. Shhhh, my god.

GREG. Why do you want to work all the time?

TAYLOR. I have a lot of lines!

GREG. You know them. Let's not rehearse. Let's never rehearse, never ever, let's leave this horrible town, I hate it here, let's start a life in Rio, I'll seduce tourists while you take their wallets, it will be everything we ever /dreamed of.

TAYLOR. Not everything is a joke.

GREG. YES IT IS! YES. IT. IS. Let's have some fun, should we bully someone?

TAYLOR. I hate fun.

GREG. Taylor. Don't take offense. But that is stupid and you are very stupid for saying that, don't take offense.

TAYLOR. When I have fun, or like *(Air quotes in some way.)* "fun," like when I do /things that people say are fun.

GREG. Why do you, *(He mimics Taylor's air quotes.)* what do you mean when you say it that way?

TAYLOR. *(Continued.)* If you let me FINISH you'll know.

GREG. I'm letting you finish I just need clarification along /the way.

TAYLOR. Greg.

GREG. TAYLOR!

TAYLOR. When I have fun, I don't have a good time. I'm just going, "oh my god I'm supposed to enjoy this and I'm not enjoying it enough, I'm wasting it, my life is going to be over and it was all bad." But like when I'm working I can just work. There isn't that pressure.

GREG. You don't have fun with me? You've never had fun when we've hung out, you're lying.

TAYLOR. I'm not /lying.

GREG. You're LYING, don't lie in front of our children.

TAYLOR. No, it's not *un*fun, but in the back of my mind is worry. All the time. It's OK, I'm used to it, it's not a problem for me. But I can't do what you do, I can't be the way that you are.

GREG. Qu'est-ce que c'est?

TAYLOR. C'est comme –

GREG. Oh no, ew, I don't actually speak French.

TAYLOR. I'm not you. I'm not like you.

GREG. You could be. With better clothes.

TAYLOR. I have too many lines to /do anything but stress.

GREG. THEN DO THEM FUN.

TAYLOR. HOW?

GREG. *(...)* Are you actually asking?

TAYLOR. I just asked.

> (**GREG** *catches the script.*)
>
> (*Carefully goes to the center of the space.*)
>
> (*Motions for* **TAYLOR** *to step back /give him room.*)
>
> (*Closes his eyes.*)
>
> (*Inhale.*)
>
> (*Go.*)

GREG. Hey hunties, it's the stage manager here, calling the calls, running the show, and making sure we don't put up a Pile. Of. Trash. You don't have time for some two-bit, cardboard, missed-lines piece of nonsense, you don't have time for no HIGH SCHOOL BULLSHIT. You came for the DRAMA. You're in Grover's Corners, the city that never sleeps, the birthplace of Rock and

Roll, the fashion capital of the world, that's right, all those other cities are LIARS, we all know that This. Is the Place. It's your town, it's my town, it's *Our Town*, it's Funkytown.

(He points to an area of the stage.)

Gibbs.

(He points to another area of the stage.)

Webbs.

(He starts voguing.)

What. What. What.

(He strikes some poses.)

Let's Begin.

(He freezes, in a stunning tableau. Hold 1, 2, 3.)

(He bows dramatically.)

(He turns to **TAYLOR**.*)*

That would be something I can relate to.

(He tosses the script.)

TAYLOR. OK –

GREG. Instead of this heteronormative garbage.

TAYLOR. But that's you, /that's not –

GREG. It's you too, /I've seen it, you just don't let it out!

TAYLOR. It's not –

GREG. *(Continued.)* THEN DO IT YOUR WAY.

TAYLOR. I don't know what /to say.

GREG. You just SAY /SOMETHING.

TAYLOR. I hate everyone in this town!

GREG. YES.

TAYLOR. They are all the most –

GREG. This is so much better already –

TAYLOR. Selfish. Boring. Self-obsessed weirdos that I've ever met.

GREG. And they have terrible hair.

TAYLOR. Every. Single. Person. In this town, blah blah blah they go, all day long. No one in this whole play ever stops and goes, "how is the stage manager?"

>   (**BECKY** *laughs.*)

>   (*Throughout this,* **TAYLOR** *starts to take more chances with how they toss the script. They start to move with more freedom.*)

"How are you today? By the way, thank you, THANK YOU for narrating /everything that we're doing."

GREG. UNGRATEFUL!

TAYLOR. "Thank you for telling us where to go and what to do, thank you for letting us be in a play!"

GREG. Oh my god, you're so having fun.

TAYLOR. *(Smiling.)* No I'm /not.

GREG. I made Taylor /have fun!

TAYLOR. You did /not!

GREG. Yes I did!

>   (**TAYLOR** *throws some pages of the script in the air.*)

TAYLOR. Woooo!

COOKIE. Is that my script?

> (**COOKIE** *appears.*)

> (**TAYLOR** *and* **GREG** *freeze. A shower of paper falls on* **TAYLOR**.)

Is that my script?

TAYLOR. No...your lines aren't circled.

COOKIE. Is there writing? On the back?

TAYLOR. Uh –

COOKIE. There's a list, on a page near the end, it's /a grocery –

TAYLOR. "Milk, spaghetti, /white sauce –"

COOKIE. That's my script, that is my script. What are you doing, you ripped it all up.

TAYLOR. I didn't, we –

> (**TAYLOR** *looks to* **GREG** *for help, but* **GREG** *has vanished.*)

COOKIE. What is your goddamn problem. You just see something that doesn't belong to you so you destroy it?

TAYLOR. Becky will get you a new one –

COOKIE. I don't want a new one. That was mine and you ruined it.

> (**COOKIE** *starts picking up the papers.* **TAYLOR** *tries to start helping.*)

DON'T.

TAYLOR. But –

COOKIE. Leave it.

TAYLOR. I, I mean –

COOKIE. LEAVE IT. You already screwed it all up, just let me do it and leave me alone. And don't ruin things that don't belong to you.

(He goes. **GREG** *emerges from the sidelines.)*

TAYLOR. What the hell, Greg?

GREG. Those hockey guys, I'm not messing around with them.

TAYLOR. But you were the one who took his script and / you were the one who threw it.

GREG. By accident, BY ACCIDENT. You were the one who threw the /pages.

TAYLOR. You abandoned me. You ABANDONED /me.

GREG. Those guys torment me. His stupid teammates? They slapped me with wet towels every time we had pool last year. They chased me around and they do the thing with the towels and then they whip me.

TAYLOR. Cookie did that?

GREG. Not him, but /all the others.

TAYLOR. Why didn't you tell me?

GREG. Because it's boring. /Because who wants to hear that.

TAYLOR. It's not boring. I do! Of course I do. You – I tell you everything. I tell you everything. And all you ever tell me is how amazing you are? And it's not Cookie doing it, he's different. /Like he's in the play.

GREG. None of them are different. Every pool class. I started changing in the toilet stall, they would come in, under the door, and drag me out, or stand on the other toilets and smack my head. One guy peed ON me when I was in the shower.

Why do you think I'm like this when I'm with you? I need to get it all out of my system when I'm with you so that none of it shows later.

TAYLOR. Cookie's gonna hate me.

GREG. Who cares.

TAYLOR. He's gonna hate me forever.

GREG. His name is Bradley Cooke, everyone calls him Cookie as if he's adorable, he's not.

TAYLOR. He's gonna think /that I'm –

GREG. Who cares about him? Who cares what anyone thinks? /I know his dad died, I know that's sad,

TAYLOR. I do. That's important to me. I know you say you don't, but I DO.

GREG. *(Continued.)* I don't care. I know that's bad but his friends hurt me. So they deserve to hurt. I don't mean that. Yes, I do. I don't know. I do mean it sometimes. And I don't care anyway because I love myself, I really do, I wouldn't change one thing about myself, I think I am so fabulous. And so fun. I am so so fun.

TAYLOR. Well, good for you, but it's not fun for anyone else around you.

(**TAYLOR** *stalks off.*)

(**GREG** *sees* **BECKY** *and puts on a show.*)

GREG. Ready for my close up, Mr. DeMille?

BECKY. Sorry I –

TAYLOR. Don't be sorry, it's fabulous. Are we starting?

BECKY. Soon. I'm just seeing where people are.

GREG. Well. I'll be right here. Just waiting to grace the stage with my presence.

BECKY. OK. Hey, Greg?

GREG. Yessss?

BECKY. Your outfit is *(Chef's kiss.)*

GREG. Hm. You should see me when I'm trying.

>*(He sashays away.)*

>*(A banging is heard.)*

BECKY. Oh god. I knew it. I knew it!

>I don't like calling everyone before they're needed. It gives them time to go away.

>>(**ANTON** *bangs on a door from outside by the field.)*

>Which DJ and Anton have done.

ANTON. Hey, can someone come out here please? It's OK, DJ.

DJ. Mm.

BECKY. They're down that hallway I talked about, and they've gone outside. Remember the outside door that sometimes locks?

DJ.	**ANTON**.
I think I'm um...argh.	Is anyone there? I know, you're OK.

BECKY. This is not a surprise; this is what DJ does.

DJ. Or every choice I've ever made in my life is wrong and nothing can ever be OK /again.

ANTON. We'll walk around the school if we have to and go in the front.

BECKY. And Anton just follows along.

DJ. That's not what I'm – OK, but –

BECKY. How can you ever get through to someone who just doesn't /give a shit?

DJ. At some point there isn't a front door that you can / walk through and then what, then you're locked outside forever, maybe I'm supposed to be locked outside, maybe that's my destiny.

ANTON. We shouldn't've done this today, I knew it. You weren't in the headspace for it and neither am I, really. *(Bang bang.)* Hello?

DJ. Shit. Shit. Shit. /Shit. Shit. Shit.

ANTON. Deej, breathe, let's go, we'll walk around and /it'll be fine and no one will know. OK, just, take a breath and –

DJ. It's not about walking around, that's not what I'm talking about –

> *(**SABREENA** opens the door.)*

> *(**DJ** and **ANTON** stare at her.)*

SABREENA. Hey.

DJ.	**ANTON**.
...Whoa.	There, you see?

SABREENA. Are you guys OK?

ANTON. Yeah, we're good. Right? We're good now, I told you it would be OK. We're fine. Thank you.

SABREENA. OK. Well.

> *(**SABREENA** goes to leave. **DJ** and **ANTON** lunge for the door.)*

DJ.	**ANTON**.
No no no no wait –	Hold on hold on hold the dooooor...

> *(**SABREENA** catches the door again.)*

(**SABREENA** *fiddles with the handle.*)

SABREENA. There. Now it's set so it won't lock.

DJ.	**ANTON**.
Genius.	Thank you.

SABREENA. It's a door. I know how doors work. Mostly. Not really though I guess if I think about it.

DJ. Hero genius. What were you doing?

SABREENA. Me? /Nothing.

DJ.	**ANTON**.
Yeah.	You're Sabreena, right?

SABREENA. I'm in the play but – wow, yeah.

DJ. Did Becky send you? To get me?

SABREENA. No. I just don't know where to be. What are you doing out here?

ANTON.	**DJ**.
You know.	Mwa ha ha ha.

(**SABREENA** *actually does not know. She genuinely has no idea.*)

DJ. You know.

(*Nope. She does not.*)

DJ.	**ANTON**.
Whoa so this is like a genuine learning opportunity, whoa. OK. OK!	Oh my goodness me.

(**DJ** *pulls out a joint from behind her back.*)

(*This is the first time* **SABREENA**'s *ever seen weed in real life.*)

SABREENA. Oh. That's. You're. Yeah. OK.

ANTON. Some people say they do their best work on it. Carl Sagan. In Silicon Valley they're all microdosing so they can think clearer and /have new ideas.

DJ. I have anxiety.

SABREENA. Oh, me too.

DJ. *(Offers* **SABREENA** *the joint.)* Aha!

SABREENA. Ha ha. I don't. Do that.

DJ. You don't, or you haven't?

SABREENA.	**ANTON**.
Both.	Oooh...

ANTON. *(Continued.)* It's like you're a little guy and this is your, you know, your, your, like, your threshold moment!

DJ. *(Sings.)*
THRESHOLD MOMENT.

ANTON. Ahh! Literally! Literally a threshold moment! Into the unknown!

> *(**DJ** and **ANTON** are so excited, they do a little "excited" dance.)*

DJ. Ahem. Come out here.

SABREENA. Really?

ANTON. You know how doors work.

SABREENA. I'm not like in the way?

DJ.	**ANTON**.
This is destiny right here.	In the way? No.

ANTON. *(Continued.)* Sometimes you die, in a game, if sometimes you go and there's something that's gonna kill you, but you have to explore, there might be gold

or something. You can refuse the call to adventure but
that's just /on the way to –

>   (**SABREENA** *just steps out.*)

>   (**ANTON** *and* **DJ** *are mad impressed.
>   They cheer.*)

Whoa you just like did it!

DJ. One of us, one of us!

SABREENA. Is it gonna make me paranoid? /Like I'm
already kinda paranoid, so –

DJ. That's a conspiracy they tell us to not do it. Even
though it's natural. It's not even as bad as alcohol.

ANTON. I mean, you also drink alcohol.

DJ. Yeah but not every day. Sugar's just as bad for you.

ANTON. And you eat /sugar.

DJ. I'm not – I'm just saying. I partake in all vices, yes.
It's the stigma, the illegality of certain substances that
I take exception to. That, my friends, is arbitrary. It
arbits the trary. The trary is arbited.

ANTON. She gets like this when it's good. She starts talking
like that. /But sometimes she gets all sad.

DJ. I wax poetic! I told you – HEY. It calms me down,
and when it's working, I start to see things the way that
they really are. And you can too. Ready?

>   (**SABREENA** *takes the joint and holds it like
>   a cigarette between her pointer and middle
>   finger.*)

ANTON. You actually hold it like this (*He demonstrates.*).

SABREENA. Oh. (*She adjusts her fingers. Then she takes a
drag and blows smoke out immediately.*)

DJ.	ANTON.
Not quite.	Suck in, and then try to like hold it. It needs to get past your mouth.

> (**SABREENA** *takes a drag and immediately coughs.*)

DJ.	ANTON.
Exactly!	Yeah, that's...that's good.

DJ. That's eeexcellent. Eeexcellent for Sabreeeeena.

> (*They pass the joint between the three of them.*)

ANTON. I had never seen it spelled that way before I met you. With an "e" instead of an "I"? You're my first Sabreeeeeena.

SABREENA. I changed it.

ANTON. What?

SABREENA. My name. When I started here I started like halfway through November of ninth grade. Because of – it doesn't matter, it's my mom. So, they took me on a lady – blah, WORDS, they took me on a tour, this tall lady with a really long neck, she kept calling me "Serena." And she handed me my timetable and my name was at the top, "Sabrina" spelled with an "i" which is how it was always spelled, which is actually my name, and I just said, "that's not how you spell my name." Because. I don't know I thought maybe she'd remember that. I thought maybe that was more interesting. And there was a thing of getting a new timetable, and everyone was fluttering all around me. And then I just liked how it looked. It looked weird. Like me.

DJ. Oh my god.

ANTON. That. Is...

SABREENA. I've never told anyone that. No one's ever asked before.

ANTON. BAD. ASS. That is really bad ass, you changed your name.

DJ. Tis. Tis bad of the ass.

(**SABREENA** *laughs a bit.*)

ANTON. You just walked out here, you just crossed the threshold, you changed your name, and you were like "I'm Sabreena with two e's and I smoke pot," that's so / badass.

DJ. Brave.

ANTON. Really brave. Seriously. It's like you didn't even think, /you just did.

SABREENA. I like never think, it's a problem.

ANTON.	**DJ**.
I think so much, I gotta do way less.	No, that's smart.

SABREENA. I'm like gonna fail pre-calculus.

ANTON. That's easy, I can help you with that.

DJ. You know I was panicking? When we were locked out?

ANTON.	**SABREENA**.
She was.	Oh, I – no.

DJ. 'Cause I knew Becky would do that thing that she does that she looks at me like I'm letting her down? But then you came and rescued us. Like you were supposed to be here.

ANTON. It's the meeting of the mentor! /OH MY GOD. And now I can... Mm hmm, mm hmm.

DJ. And all that stuff I was – I was thinking everything I had ever done was wrong, like everything that Becky thinks about how I'm such a, I don't know, "lost cause," or like when people say I'm throwing away my potential, I thought that was all true, but it was just part of the journey. I needed to be sitting here so I could meet you so you could tell me the secret of the universe. I had to trust that someone would open the door.

God. The world is so amazing sometimes.

(*They all look at the world.*)

ANTON. We should do this every rehearsal.

(**BECKY** *looks at them. She looks at the audience.*)

BECKY. Um. I didn't... Let's go inside. We're getting close to being able to start.

Claire, Allison, Emily, and Greg are in the makeup room.

(**CLAIRE**, **ALLISON**, **EMILY**, *and* **GREG** *are in the makeup room.* **EMILY** *is doing biology homework.*)

(**CLAIRE** *and* **ALLISON** *have been trying to run lines while* **ALLISON** *puts on makeup in the mirror.* **ALLISON** *knows about makeup and is taking her time.*)

CLAIRE. So can we go again or –

ALLISON.	**GREG**.
That is an interesting question.	Everyone is way too pent up about lines around here.

ALLISON. I feel maybe the moment has passed. /Perchance?

GREG. It has absolutely passed. Now the moment is glamour. /Now the moment is seduction.

(**GREG** *elbows* **ALLISON**. **ALLISON** *shimmies.*)

CLAIRE. K, well I'll...

> *(What will Claire do? Claire doesn't know.*
> *She pat pat pats her face. To* **EMILY***:)*

Do you wanna...?

EMILY. I'm fine here.

> (**EMILY** *makes a motion like: stop with*
> *the face.)*

GREG.	CLAIRE.
Who should I seduce?	*But it hurts. Wahh.*
(To **ALLISON***.)* I'll leave	
Will for you.	

ALLISON. Or whoever. I can also just find a random sailor
while I'm walking the streets.

> (**ALLISON** *begins to dance a dance of*
> *seduction.)*

GREG. Wow you're so much like your character, that's such
an Emily thing /to say.

ALLISON. I know!

> (**EMILY** *looks up.)*

EMILY. Not me. Right. It's never me.

GREG.	CLAIRE.
(To **EMILY***.)* You don't	Always you. Hey.
really seem like the	
random sailor type.	

ALLISON. Oh I don't know, I think our Emily, real Emily,
might have a certain suitor, dah dahhh...

EMILY.	CLAIRE.
STOP! I don't. No one.	What? Who?
No one!	

ALLISON. Mmm, I'll never tell, I am sworn to secrecy.

GREG. WAAAAIIITT, who does Claire like?

> *(They all look at* **CLAIRE**. **CLAIRE** *makes a laugh sound that doesn't really come out like a laugh.)*

CLAIRE. Hnnh. Hiyin ooah. Uh. I don't like anyone. I'm like a… Farmer.

ALLISON.	**GREG**.
(To **CLAIRE**.*)* Can I put makeup on you?	What?

CLAIRE. No. That's OK, /I don't –

GREG. Ooh. I don't know if I've ever seen you wear makeup.

CLAIRE. I wear makeup.

GREG.	**EMILY**.
Really? But this will be like glam, I've never seen you glam.	No you don't.

CLAIRE. Just not on the days that I have to swim, /I really don't –

EMILY. You swim every day though.

CLAIRE. I swim Monday and Wednesday mornings and Tuesday and Thursday after school, /I don't do it the mornings I have practice, what would be the point. You know when I swim.

GREG. Ugh I'd kill myself if I had to swim every Monday and Wednesday morning, I'd just kill myself.

> *(***EMILY*** shrugs.)*

CLAIRE. Mrowr?

GREG. K, I'm bored, I'm doing you then.

(**GREG** *starts putting makeup onto one of*
EMILY's *limbs.*)

CLAIRE. Oh, she doesn't like that. Emily. Emily.

EMILY. It's fine, I don't mind.

CLAIRE. You hate when there's like anything dirty on you.

ALLISON.	**GREG.**
You do? Ooh, I write on you all the time in bio.	It's not dirt, it's beauty.

EMILY.	**CLAIRE.**
I don't.	You like can't stand it, what are you –?

ALLISON. Maybe I should stop invading your personal space. /But the problem is that I love invading your personal space and won't stop doing it.

EMILY. No, I don't want to get through bio without that, I love when you write on me. I loved when you drew me as a quadratic equation.

ALLISON.	**CLAIRE.**
That was my best one.	A what?

EMILY. She drew me as, /you know the quadratic equation?

ALLISON. This isn't going to make sense to someone who wasn't there. I just wrote out the quadratic equation on her arm and put her face /at the top of the ax-squared.

EMILY. With a bubble saying, "I'm Emily the Quadratic Equation."

CLAIRE. Oh. But /you hate that.

GREG. I'm NOT doing that. Is that what you're doing in your smart person classes? /This would be better if you – put the book down.

ALLISON. I don't know, I'm mostly sitting there singing show tunes in my head.

EMILY. No, I – we have a test tomorrow.

GREG. You don't see Allison studying for it.

CLAIRE.	**ALLISON.**
You've memorized that textbook, anyway.	The mitochondria is the powerhouse of the cell.

EMILY. I have not.

CLAIRE. You have. You told me you memorized the textbook over the summer.

ALLISON. ...Have you actually memorized the textbook?

EMILY. ...No –

CLAIRE.	**GREG.**
She has.	Oh my god.

EMILY. Claire.

ALLISON. Did you know the mitochondria is the powerhouse /of the cell?

CLAIRE. What, you have, that's impressive.

ALLISON. That's why I sit next to you and copy off of you.

EMILY. I haven't really memorized it, if /I had memorized it why would I have to study now?

ALLISON. I don't copy. I don't know why I said that, I've never done anything like that in my life, I'm terrified to ever get in trouble. I sit next to you because /I love you num num num.

(**ALLISON** *eats* **EMILY**'s *face.*)

GREG. Are you going to be a doctor, Emily?

CLAIRE.	**EMILY.**
Yes she is. WHAT?	I don't know.

EMILY. Don't say that, I don't know if I will be.

ALLISON. You would excel at that. As you do all things.

EMILY. You need to have really good grades. /Thanks.

CLAIRE. You HAVE really good grades.

EMILY. I have...OK grades.

CLAIRE.	**GREG**.
You get /all 90s.	I don't even read the books they assign.

EMILY. I'm saying I do OK. Can I have /my book back please?

CLAIRE. But you don't do "OK," you do "amazing," so just say that. Who are you being right now, /what is this?

EMILY. What?

GREG. I threw *Ethan Frome* out the window, /I hated that book.

ALLISON. Oh I loved *Ethan* – oh. /Ha ha! Nevermind.

> (**MARY** *comes in – not expecting for people to be in here.*)

EMILY. You need to be so good to do anything though now, that's all I'm saying. Like. The bar is on the roof, it's so hard. So. And extra-curriculars. You have to just be perfect at everything.

ALLISON. "Now, now, nobody's perfect."*(She sees* **MARY**.*)* / Mary, my angel, from heaven!

EMILY. But you have to be.

GREG. *(To* **ALLISON**.*)* You're pretty perfect. Will thinks you're pretty perfect.

EMILY.	**ALLISON**.
And I know nobody is – you actually are, Allison.	Aw.

EMILY. I'm not, but you have to be.

    (**MARY** *leaves.)*

ALLISON. I'm a dirty trollop.

EMILY. You know I saw this thing that said your personal essay for college? People who judge the essays said, "We've heard every trauma." There's no way to be good enough. There's no way to compete if you're not a complete /like...superstar.

GREG. Then fuck that school.

CLAIRE. That's Harvard, you can't fuck Harvard.

GREG. I could fuck Harvard.

ALLISON.	**CLAIRE**.
I believe in you, Greg.	It's her dream school and she's going to go.

GREG.	**EMILY**.
Thank you, I believe in myself.	Claire!

CLAIRE. It is, that's /awesome.

EMILY. When I was like ten, I don't, I mean –

CLAIRE. It's your dream.

EMILY. I don't know – don't say that.

    It's just like very very hard. Not everyone makes it. And then what.

ALLISON. But /you're very very smart.

CLAIRE. But you're – you are and it also comes naturally to you. You don't even have to work hard to get amazing grades.

EMILY. I work really hard. /You know how –

CLAIRE. But you don't have to.

EMILY. Yes I do, of course I...I don't know the future, all right? And I want a future. I don't know what future, but I... and it's not guaranteed, my cousin is the smartest person I know and she has a Master's and she can't get a job and she cries all the time. And it's harder for us than our parents. That's a fact. We have to grow up and accept that, /that's real.

CLAIRE. Your grades are already – I'm grown up – your grades are amazing and you don't even need a scholarship to go anywhere you want because your parents will just pay for it. Like. If you want to be real. If you want to grow up, then just be honest and admit that. Just like...

(Beat.)

ALLISON. *(Singing a made-up song.)*
"EVERYONE'S PERFECT IN THEIR OWN WAY"

GREG. *(Re: makeup.)* Yes. But we all need a little help. A little zhuzh. Claire...

CLAIRE. I don't feel like it.	**ALLISON.** *(Gasp.)* Yessssssss.

GREG. Mwahaha, time for glamor.	**EMILY.** Yeah, she needs a makeover.

*(**GREG** and **ALLISON** advance on **CLAIRE**.)*

CLAIRE. No, I don't want it.

ALLISON. Please, it'll be fun.	**EMILY.** Let them do it, it'll look good.

GREG. We'll do a very simple day-to-night look.

EMILY. Come on, Claire, just –

CLAIRE. NO!

GREG. Whoa.

CLAIRE. Sorry.

GREG. You can /chill.

CLAIRE. I just don't want to. 'Cause of my...sorry.

ALLISON. It's not bad. I wouldn't have noticed if you didn't say anything.

CLAIRE. It hurts.

GREG. There's Accutane.

CLAIRE.	**EMILY**.
I tried that.	She already tried it.

GREG. My sister, my half-sister, had really bad acne but now she's normal. She bought this makeup online that covers everything, /it's like a sharpie for your face.

ALLISON. I get zits all the time.

CLAIRE. That is – that's not the same.

EMILY. It's really not that /bad, Claire.

GREG.	**CLAIRE**.
It's totally not –	Yes it is! I have eyes, I look in the mirror, OK?

EMILY. Then you should know that you're beautiful.

CLAIRE. Oh my god.

ALLISON.	**GREG**.	**EMILY**.
You're so pretty.	You have such pretty hair.	You are.

CLAIRE. Emily, shut up. Stop pretending.

EMILY. I'm /not.

CLAIRE. Yes you are. It's not nice, it's not – it's like you think I'm stupid. Like that I don't know what I look like, I know, OK? And I'm fine with it, it's just how things are, some people get things and some people don't, and that's just how it is, and I'm fine with it but it's not nice to lie right to my face. It doesn't help me.

EMILY. I'm not lying to you.

CLAIRE. You are! I know what I am/ so don't say that –

EMILY. You're beautiful to me.

CLAIRE. I don't know why we're not allowed to talk about how you're brilliant and going to go to Harvard and have this incredible life, which is going to happen, like, there's no doubt, but then you get to lie to me about stuff that will never happen for me. I do know my future. I see it, I see people on the bus who have faces like me and they're alone, and nothing good will ever happen to them, that's the way the world is, I can't change that. And I'm fine with it, but...you know you and I are like really different, right? Like we have nothing in common so you can't understand. No matter how smart you are, you...

(A silence.)

*(**ALLISON** stands up suddenly.)*

*(**ALLISON** does a wild pantomime as if she is taking off clothes and putting other clothes on.)*

GREG. Uh.

ALLISON. Gotta practice my quick change.

GREG. What?

ALLISON. MY QUICK CHANGE! Claire, you should do this too, we will both have to change for the wedding, we need to move like lightning.

GREG. Are you wearing a parachute?

ALLISON. Like lightning! I always wear a parachute under my costume. In case the play explodes. Lightning!

GREG. Smart. Don't forget your pantyhose. Actually, I should do my pantyhose, I'm wearing several pairs.

ALLISON. Extra support.

GREG. Exactly.

> (**GREG** *joins* **ALLISON**.)

> (*They mime costumes that are ridiculous: zippers. Corsets. Elaborate headpieces.*)

Quick. Change. Quick. Change!

GREG & ALLISON. Quick. Change. Quick. Change! Quick! CHANGE! QUICK! CHANGE!

> (*They quick change.*)

> (**EMILY** *and* **CLAIRE** *stare at each other.*)

> (**EMILY** *gets up and joins the quick change.*)

> (**CLAIRE** *pats her face.*)

ALLISON. YES!

> (**SABREENA** *enters.*)

SABREENA. I'm Sabreena with two e's and I smoked pot.

ALLISON.	**EMILY**.	**GREG**.
What. Now?	You did?	Someone has pot?

SABREENA. But it didn't do anything. I smoked with them but I didn't feel anything.

GREG.	**ALLISON**.
Whhhhaaaaaaaat?	Did you inhale?

SABREENA. Yeah.

> (**ALLISON** *looks in* **SABREENA**'s *eyes.*)

ALLISON.	GREG.	EMILY.
Maybe it just didn't take.	Like really inhale?	Do you have the munchies?

SABREENA. How does everyone know so much about this?

ALLISON.	EMILY.
Life.	We studied it in heal– life.

SABREENA. Isn't it supposed to feel like more?

ALLISON. It makes me feel /really relaxed and happy JINX!

GREG. Like relaxed and happy AHHHHHH JINX YOU OWE ME A COKE.

EMILY.

Yeah that's what they /say   *(ALLISON hands GREG*
it's supposed to do.   *a mime Coke.)*

GREG. A *real* Coke.

(He grabs ALLISON's hand.)

What's that on your arm?

ALLISON.	SABREENA.
Nothing.	I don't feel anything.

EMILY. It might hit you all at once later.

ALLISON. I'm jinxed remember?

SABREENA. What happens then?

GREG. Right, you can't talk anymore, I'm Emily now.

EMILY. *(Hearing her name.)* What? /Oh. I want my name back!

GREG. I'm Emily now, YOU CAN'T, NOW THAT'S /ME!

SABREENA. What happens when it hits me?

GREG. You turn into a lizard.

ALLISON.   **EMILY.**
  Probably nothing. Don't   It depends.
  PUNCH!

SABREENA. Oh I'd love to be a lizard, chameleons hold
  anything you give them.

GREG. *(Miming, while wresting with* **ALLISON***.)* Oh here.

SABREENA. What is that?

GREG. Coke.

SABREENA. COCAINE?

GREG.   **ALLISON.**   **EMILY.**
  What?   Greg, get off!   Guys, we're
                                              being loud.

SABREENA. Is this another thing that is supposed to be a
  thing but it isn't? Like everyone says it's a big deal and
  then you do it and it's like "oh." Is everything like that?

GREG. Blow jobs are.

EMILY.   **ALLISON.**   **SABREENA.**
  Oh my god.   Ha.   Well that's not
                                              surprising.

GREG. *(Punches* **ALLISON** *in the arm.)* You broke Jinx,
  where is my real genuine life Coca-Cola?

ALLISON. Ow!

EMILY. How does a blow job even work?

        (They all look at her.)

  I mean –

GREG.   **ALLISON.**
  Ohhh, you're a   Awwww!
  bayyybeeee!

BECKY. And then Ms. Welles was finally ready.

> (**BECKY** *plays* **MS. WELLES** *and walks onto the stage.*)

OK, everyone, let's gather please, everyone to the stage please.

> (*Everyone moves to the stage, severally.*)

OK, this is the wedding scene, everyone, the wedding scene, so we need to make a wedding. Now Emily, / we're going to have you enter –

EMILY. Yes? Oh. /AHHHHHH!

BECKY AS MS. WELLES. Character Emily, excuse me, we're going to have you enter through here.	**GREG.** Not you.

> (**CLAIRE** *hugs* **EMILY**.)

DJ. I should probably give her away, right?	**CLAIRE.** You're my only Emily. You're the only Emily I'll ever have.

BECKY AS MS. WELLES. Yes, that would be great, go do that.	**EMILY.** Are we OK?

DJ. (*To* **ALLISON**.) Daughter.	**CLAIRE.** Yeah.

ALLISON. Father. Wait, I want Claire, can both my parents give me away?

GREG.	**DJ.**
Ooh modern!	My sister did that at her wedding.

MARY. Oh I love that.

BECKY AS MS. WELLES.	**DJ.**
I don't know...	Yeah, my mom was really proud.

ALLISON.	**ANTON.**
Please?	That's more us. Like. Representative.

TAYLOR. Yeah, who cares how it's supposed to be, this should be our /show.

ANTON.	**GREG.**
Yeah!	It's *Our Town*, bitches!

REID.	**MARY.**
I'll give her away, that would be most natural. I'm joking.	A new Grover's Corners!

>   (**SAM** *laughs at* **REID.**)

ALL. *(Severally.)* Please Wellesy?, Let Claire do it!, We should try it! etc.

BECKY AS MS. WELLES. Fine, we'll try it, we'll try it. Let's have all the Gibbs on stage right, /and all the Webbs on stage left.

WILL. *(To* **MARY.***)* My dear?

>   (**MARY** *and* **WILL** *link arms.*)

BECKY AS MS. WELLES. *(Continued.)* George, you stand here. And Taylor, you're marrying them, so you'll be in the middle, that's right.

(Everyone makes a tableau while she talks.)

ANTON. Where would I be? I think I know both families.

EMILY.	**COOKIE.**
Yeah, me too.	I don't know where to go.

BECKY AS MS. WELLES. Just, pick a side if you aren't in one of the families. /Fill in a little more.

REID. Wait, shouldn't there be the horse?

(The hubbub calms. Did we hear that right?)

Who has the horse?

ANTON. *(Raising his hand.)* Uh... Howie Newsome.

REID. Shouldn't that like /be here too.

ANTON. I don't think I'd bring my /horse to a wedding.

CLAIRE. Why would a horse come to a wedding?

ANTON.	**GREG.**
It would take up four seats.	It's a very romantic horse.

*(**DJ** makes a horse sound.)*

REID. But shouldn't we use the horse? Don't we want to show off the horse?

(There's a weird beat.)

MARY. But it's not a real horse. It's all imaginary. Right? It says so in the script. So.

*(Beat. **REID** realizes he has made a terrible error.)*

REID. No, I know.

WILL. Wait. Did you think we were going to get a real horse?

(This strikes **SABREENA** *as deeply funny. She smiles a goofy smile.)*

REID. No! I just thought – never mind.

WILL.	**TAYLOR.**
Oh, /Reid.	Ohhhhhhh...

REID.	**ALLISON.**
Nothing, nothing, /nothing!	Oh my god!

ANTON. We like don't even have a set. /How could we have a horse?

*(***SABREENA*** starts giggling.)*

CLAIRE. Wait, I thought there was no set.

EMILY.	**TAYLOR.**
There isn't, that's what he said.	There's no nothing.

DJ. My daughter can't get married without a horse.

*(***SABREENA*** can't take it.)*

TAYLOR. There's no horse, there's no props.

SABREENA. Where are we going to get a horse? WHERE ARE WE GOING TO GET A HORSE?

*(***SABREENA*** falls on the floor.)*

MARY.	**ALLISON.**
Oh my god.	Whoa, are you OK?

*(***SABREENA*** puts her legs up in the air.)*

SABREENA.   WHERE ARE WE GOING TO GET A HORSE?

ANTON.	**EMILY.**

From a horse store.   My cousin has a horse.

COOKIE. "Bring in the horse!"

> *(Everyone is shocked/delighted that* **COOKIE** *is participating. Some others start to giggle.)*

ANTON. *(Pretending to be a truck backing up, bringing in a horse.)* Beep...beep...beep...

SABREENA. I'm sorry. I'M SORRY. IT HURTS. *(She laughs.)* IT HURTS TO LAUGH.

DJ. It hit her! It totally hit her!

> *(***ANTON** *and* **DJ** *high five.)*

> *(***SABREENA** *alternates between laughing and moaning.)*

> *(The laughter starts rippling through the others. They are mostly laughing at* **SABREENA.***)*

> *(Others start to echo her moans.)*

BECKY AS MS. WELLES. OK, let's get it together.

WILL. Like, if we get a horse, /it has to be in every scene.

BECKY AS MS. WELLES. THERE'S NO HORSE.

REID.   **MARY.**
  I'm such an idiot.   Like when we're walking?

SAM.   **WILL.**
  No, you're not.   IT'S SMELLING THE
                                       HELIOTROPE.

> *(People pat* **REID** *on the back.)*

WILL & MARY. "IN THE MOONLIGHT!"

(**WILL** *does his heel clicky, picking-the-heliotrope thing.*)

DJ. WAIT WAIT WAIT. THE HORSE IS THE MAYOR OF THE TOWN.

(*The crowd goes wild.*)

BECKY AS MS. WELLES.	EMILY.
All right, all right, everyone, let's settle.	MAYOR HORSE!

EMILY. MAYOR HORSE! MAYOR HORSE!

(**DJ** *stamps and shakes her mane out like a filly.*)

(**COOKIE** *bends and holds* **DJ***'s waist, becoming the back half – and boom, we have a horse, magic of theatre.*)

(*The fake horse makes sounds and prances.*)

(**ANTON** *walks him as Howie Newsome.*)

(**TAYLOR** *throws pages of their script in celebration.*)

(**GREG** *vogues.*)

(*Some people have never seen* **EMILY** *so excited and they laugh at that.*)

(*Others join the chant, it's like "Quick Change" before.*)

GREG, EMILY & SAM. MAYOR HORSE! MAYOR HORSE!

(*It's pandemonium.*)

(*They are all laughing so much.*)

(*Insane, giddy cheers.*)

BECKY AS MS. WELLES. Please, everyone! We have to get through this!

> (**BECKY** *turns to the audience, and immediately:)*

ACT TWO

BECKY. It's a month later.

(*Everyone does a vocal warm-up.*)

(*Some people shake and touch their toes.*)

(*Costume elements might appear, but maybe not.*)

(*Slight manic backstage energy leaking out of everyone.*)

I told my parents to come tomorrow because I didn't want them to come to opening. Because for sure something will go wrong.

COOKIE. I can't find my pants. For the show.

BECKY. Seriously?

(**COOKIE** *shrugs, feels terrible.*)

I'll look. Where did you last have them? /Half an hour, everyone!

COOKIE. I...

ALL. (*Off, severally.*) Half an hour, thank you; Ahhhh! Oh my God! I need to do my makeup! etc.

BECKY. Allison is in the stairwell. The pre-backstage that I told you about? Mary's backstage right, I saw Sam, everyone's everywhere. Where are Cookie's pants?!

(**ALLISON** *is in the stairwell, staring into the wings.*)

(**WILL** *comes up behind her.*)

WILL. Hey.

(**ALLISON** *looks at him.*)

ALLISON. Oh. /Hi.

WILL. Sorry. Didn't mean to startle you. /Are you like – do you want to be alone?

ALLISON. That's OK, I – no. No. I'm just running the lines.

(**MARY**, *backstage right, listens.* **WILL** *and* **ALLISON** *don't see her.*)

WILL. We just have to have fun. That's the most important thing.

ALLISON. Is it?

WILL. *(Mystified.)* Yeah. /Of course it is?

ALLISON. I wasn't nervous until now. I really thought it would be like nothing. But it's really scary! There's like people out there! And this is what we've been working for! For a really long time! I didn't really think about that. /It's crazy.

WILL. Would you go out with me – Sorry, I didn't mean to interrupt you, that's rude but /I –

ALLISON. Yes.

WILL. Really?

ALLISON. Like on a /date?

WILL. Ugh. That's awesome! Yeah, a date. Well I was gonna ask you to go to homecoming with me. The dance. If you want. But we should go on a date before that.

ALLISON. Uh. OK.

WILL. Yeah?

ALLISON. Yeah.

>*(WILL and ALLISON hug.)*

Shit, I forgot about the play! What if all my lines left my brain?

WILL. Here.

>*(WILL picks up lines that fell out of ALLISON's brain.)*
>
>*(He puts them back in her head.)*
>
>*(They disappear from our view.)*
>
>*(MARY moves to the stairwell.)*
>
>*(She starts to cry.)*
>
>*(She suddenly slaps herself violently across the face.)*

MARY. Shut up you idiot.

>*(MARY smacks her brain.)*

ANTON. Mary?

>*(ANTON appears in the stairwell.)*

You OK?

MARY. *(Nods, yeah yeah cool cool.)* Nervous.

ANTON. Me too. I keep thinking my pants are going to fall down. When I bend over to do the thing with the horse?

MARY. Are they too big?

ANTON. No, they fit. I'm just worried they'll fall down. Cookie lost his though. We can't find them anywhere.

(**ANTON** *starts to leave and then turns around back to* **MARY**.)

I just wanted to say. I think you're doing a really good job in the play.

(**MARY** *looks at him.*)

Every time you're in a scene I just watch you. And I heard Wellesy saying, it was when you and Will were doing your walking scene, she said, "Mary's really an actor." So. Everyone knows that. We all talk about how good you are. You might just not hear it. Sometimes I think something but I don't want to think it because I'm afraid it will jinx me or something? So maybe you don't want to think it. I don't want to jinx you – shit – I don't want to jinx you right before the show if you like need to think you're bad or something. Do you do that?

Sometimes I do that. Like. Uh. Try to tell myself that I'm bad so I work harder so that I can be good. Like motivate? With games and stuff, when I do a hard part I'll be like, "I suck, I suck." So I get it. But maybe you don't have to do that. 'Cause you're really good anyway. Really good. Like. Amazing.

Yeah. Um. Good luck.

(**ANTON** *starts to go.*)

Oh no! You're /not supposed to say it.

MARY. It's OK.

ANTON. It's like Ahhh.

(*He mimes something falling on him from above.*)

Now a bunch of terrible stuff's gonna happen.

MARY. Oh my god, /well don't say that!

MARY. I'm just kidding, I'm just kidding. Break a leg. You're. You're awesome.

BECKY. *(Into her headset.)* Ten minutes to curtain, everyone, house is open!

ACTORS. *(Severally – not all of them remember and it's not in unison.)* Thanks, ten!, Thank you, ten!, Ahhhhh!

TAYLOR. Becky?

BECKY. Hi. Are you OK?

TAYLOR. Yeah. No. Ha ha ha! /I just wanted to say –

BECKY. Yeah.

TAYLOR. It's really hard to be the Stage Manager. And. You're doing a really good job. So. Thank you.

> *(They look at each other.)*

> *(They hug fiercely.)*

BECKY. *(Into her headset.)* Everyone to the drama room.

> *(They are all in the drama room.* **BECKY** *becomes* **MS. WELLES**.*)*

BECKY AS MS. WELLES. All right everyone, this is...this is it.

I just want to thank you so much for your hard work. I'm so proud of you all.

DJ. Wellesy...

BECKY AS MS. WELLES. What?

DJ. I don't want to cry.

BECKY AS MS. WELLES. OK, OK. But I am. Um. You'll be great. Stay calm. Help each other. Things might change, and things might go wrong, but it's OK.

I'm just going to say one tiny thing. The first time that I saw a play – it was *Peter Pan* –

(There are "awws" of recognition.)

Yes, and seeing that...it was the closest I had ever come to magic. And the first time I did a play – and it was *Our Town* –

DJ. Oh, wow.

BECKY AS MS. WELLES. – It was the closest I had come, at that point in my life, to feeling like I had friends. So. It's magic. And your friends are in the theatre. That's why people come. That's why I teach it, that's why we do it, we do it so we can see our friends.

Now you guys will do something as a cast. Like a bonding thing. I'm gonna leave you and you'll do something and that will be your cast thing, and you'll never tell anyone outside this room what it is. OK? I will see you all after. Everybody listen to Becky. Oh DJ.

DJ. I'm fine. I'm fine. That was amazing.

ALL. *(Severally.)* Thank you, we love you, See you after, etc.

> *(**MS. WELLES** leaves.)*
>
> *(**BECKY** watches from the sidelines.)*
>
> *(Everyone looks at each other for a second. Ooh. What will we do?)*
>
> *(**MARY** holds out her hands, as if to form a circle.)*
>
> *(They all hold hands in a circle.)*
>
> *(**SAM** and **REID** are next to each other – maybe with some maneuvering done by **REID**.)*
>
> *(**WILL** and **ALLISON** are next to each other, which **MARY** notices.)*

WILL. Let's turn out the lights.

(**BECKY** *turns out the lights – they are still visible.*)

(*There are some giggles. Someone goes "oooh."*)

(*Then it gets very quiet.*)

ALLISON. Let's pass a squeeze. I'll start.

(*They pass a squeeze in silence.*)

(*At some point during the circle squeeze, **SAM** starts to sing a song.*)

(*The cast should pick this song.*)

(*Not everyone has to know the words.*)

(*But people start joining in.*)

(*If it's fast-paced, they might dance a bit.*)

(*They sing the instrumental parts. They make the song actually come alive.*)

(*And at the height of the song, it suspends, unfinished and –*)

BECKY. The curtain went up at seven thirty-six, to allow for late comers. I missed four cues. One I'm sure everyone noticed. The others probably not.

My parents saw it the next night and said that it was too long but very good.

We did three performances and sold out all four hundred and fifty tickets, plus standing room every night.

It was a pretty good show, you know?

ACT THREE

BECKY. I guess you all know what happened next. Lot of coverage.

I didn't know how to do this part. But. I mean why else did I...?

There's a line in the play that Grover's Corners – that's the place in *Our Town* – likes facts. So.

Six weeks later. Homecoming's on a Saturday, and it's in the gym. The dance is at eight.

He comes in through the doors down the hallway from the drama department. Sometimes they lock. This time they open. He walks down the hallway. Through the drama room, past the little makeup room. Down the stairs, the little – you know this, I already told you this. He enters stage right. He walks right through where I am now. Out that way to the lobby. To get to the rest of the school.

And into the gym. Where everyone is.

He's wearing camo pants and big black boots. Like he looks the way...he looks how you think they look. I guess they copy each other. It's a thing.

At first people don't hear it. Because the music? And it's crowded so people don't really see, or don't understand what's happening.

I'm on the other side of the room and all I hear is screaming, and then I'm being pushed, I'm being pushed by so many people.

SABREENA. At first, I'm pissed.

CLAIRE. I had to go to the bathroom.

SABREENA.   **REID.**
Like "why are you   Chill out, everyone.
pushing?"

ANTON. I drank before. And I had been panicking that a
teacher was going to be able to tell.

EMILY. Claire had to go to the bathroom and we were
going to meet /near the change rooms after.

DJ. Anton and I drank.

ANTON. Why do I do stuff I don't want to do?

TAYLOR. The gym was all silver and blue. It actually
looked really nice.

WILL. We had said we'd go as a group.

MARY. I'm there with Anton.

WILL. I'm there with Allison.

CLAIRE.   **EMILY.**
Everyone's there.   Claire looked so pretty.

TAYLOR. Greg and I still aren't speaking.

SAM. I was on the other side of the gym, /I was talking to
my brother and his friends.

COOKIE. My mom said I should go. I didn't want to. She
said I should try to get back to normal. But like a dance
isn't normal. A dance is high pressure.

MARY. They're playing this old song, this –

DJ. "Everybody dance now."

REID. They were playing crap music all night.

ANTON. DJ was joking it was the DJ from a /Bar Mitzvah.

DJ. DUN. DUN DUN DUN DUN.

(**SABREENA** *clamps her hands over her ears at the first sound of the song.*)

MARY. So dorky.

TAYLOR. I had a moment like, "Oh, I'm actually having fun."

GREG. Mary and I are having a dance fight. Taylor looks like they're having a really good time.

DJ. It's weird 'cause in that song the woman's almost screaming.

GREG. And I'm like, is that to prove something to me?

TAYLOR. Like I saw myself, as if I was watching myself in a movie, and I was smiling. /I was having fun.

WILL. It's so loud. The shot.

GREG. I'm going to win the dance fight. Obvi.

BECKY. And then –

GREG. I'm going to destroy the competition.

COOKIE. BANG.

ANTON. When it happens, it's loud.

TAYLOR. A gunshot doesn't sound like anything else. It's like your body knows that it's /dangerous.

MARY. I get this ringing in my ear, and then it's like we're in a bubble or /something.

ANTON. And I'm such a – god, I'm so stupid I think, "They know! They know I have a flask! They're going to expel me!"

COOKIE. But you're like how can it be a gunshot? A gunshot isn't something that you hear.

WILL. I knew immediately.

COOKIE. Here?

ANTON. 'Cause the worst thing would be /to be expelled.

CLAIRE. In the bathroom, everyone suddenly freezes. /And we're like, "what?"

REID. Part of me was like "there's no way."

SAM. One of them was telling me about this theory he had about *Lord of the Rings* /and I heard it but he wouldn't stop talking, and I was worried but didn't want to interrupt him.

WILL. And it made me sad that I knew immediately, because like that isn't something we should know.

COOKIE. It takes you a second to /put all the information together.

DJ. I used to have a dream about something like this.

SAM. Oh no, it's happening again.

COOKIE. BANG. BANG BANG /BANG.

GREG. There's this burning pain /in my leg.

DJ. But it was in the building that I took karate in when I was a kid.

SAM. I grabbed my brother's hand.

REID. I just keep thinking, "Not in the spine. Please don't get me in my spine."

MARY.	**SAM.**
I see Will.	This time we know what to do.

TAYLOR. And then it is panic.

MARY.	**GREG.**
I see the whites of his eyes.	On the side of my thigh.

     (**MARY** *starts to walk forward.*)

COOKIE. When there's more, everyone realizes what it is.

DJ. But I would have it with people who weren't in karate with me.

SAM.	**CLAIRE**.
I never ran so fast in my life.	And then it's like everyone had rehearsed it in their minds.

DJ. Dreams, man.

EMILY. I get under a table.

TAYLOR. Like, I was right about fun.

ANTON. Mary?

TAYLOR. It can't last.

> (**TAYLOR** *starts to walk forward.*)

SAM. After I'm like I ran so fast.

ANTON. MARY!

WILL. Mary looks at me and she looks worried, /but I don't know what her worried look means and then –

DJ. We would run away from one guy and step out of the elevator and another guy would be there.

> (**WILL** *starts to walk forward.*)

EMILY. I pull all the chairs in around /and I hide in the middle of the table.

CLAIRE. There are like twenty girls in this tiny bathroom, and we hear shots. /And we stand on the toilets, trying to hide.

SAM. I am all the way to the corner before I stop.

GREG.	**ANTON**.
It hurts more than you can imagine.	I am holding Mary's hand.

SABREENA. I think of my mom and I just feel guilty.

DJ. He would blow someone's jaw off.

SAM. And then I run all the way /home.

COOKIE.	**GREG**.
BANG.	And then it goes numb.

EMILY. I had been so worried about my dress.

CLAIRE. Like twenty of us trying to stand /on four toilets.

SABREENA. I see all this red coming out from under a table.

ANTON. I keep thinking as long as I hold her hand /she can't go.

EMILY. That it was the wrong color, that it looked stupid, that someone else would have the same one, that everyone else /always looks so much better than me.

REID. One of the guns was his dad's. He had a permit for it. They later found out /he used a fake ID to get the other ones he had on him from a Walmart out of town.

GREG. And I start thinking, "I'm not going to walk."

EMILY. Like there are some people who just look good no matter what and the rest of us can't compete with that.

(**EMILY** *starts to walk forward.*)

SABREENA. He also had some explosives on him. They said he learned how to make those online. But he didn't get to use them.

GREG. And then I start thinking, "Oh, I'm going to die."

COOKIE. People's cell phones are going off. And I know it's their parents. /And their parents are just going to call and call and not get picked up.

ANTON. And I realize that in all the games I play you always move on after someone is dead, /you don't see them.

CLAIRE. I want to find Emily. This policeman tells me

REID AS POLICEMAN. "You have to /leave."

ANTON. You're just on to the next part of the /game.

COOKIE. Later, when we're in lockdown –

CLAIRE. But I can't find my friend.

COOKIE. All I can think is I miss my dad.

ANTON. And I think all these games I love are so stupid, / that's not how it is at all.

REID AS POLICEMAN. "Ma'am you have /to leave."

CLAIRE. I'm not a ma'am, and I can't. Find. My friend.

> (**BECKY** *pauses for a moment.*)

BECKY. In the end there are eight. Deceased.

It wasn't even the biggest shooting that spring.

And now it's a year later.

Honestly, the stuff that bugs me the most is all the stuff that hasn't changed. Like. I have Calc this year in the room Emily and I had Algebra last year. And the other day the desk she used to sit in was empty. And it's like, "why do we still have to have that desk? Why... How is the room the same?"

> (**ALLISON** *slowly walks in towards* **MARY**, **WILL**, **EMILY**, *and* **TAYLOR**.)

> (*She's escorted by* **MR. COOKE**, *who is played by the actor who played* **COOKIE**.)

MARY. Who's there?

MR. COOKE. It's all right, everyone, don't panic. I have someone here for you.

ALLISON. It's me. Mary?

MARY. Allison.

BECKY. Allison? But –

ALLISON. Hey.

TAYLOR. Hi Mr. Cooke.

MR. COOKE. Hey guys. You'll all make sure she's taken care of, won't you? You remember what I did when you first showed up?

　　　　(They nod.)

All right. Be good. I know you're good, but. Be good.

　　　　(He goes.)

ALLISON. *(Gasps.)* Oh, I know who that is now.

MARY. What happened?

ALLISON. I just um... *(She shakes her head.)*

MARY. Oh no. Will. Allison's here.

WILL. Hi Allison.

ALLISON. Hi Will. Hi Emily. Hi Taylor. Oh wow. It's you guys.

EMILY. What are you...why are you... /oh my god.

WILL. Was there another one? Did it happen again?

ALLISON. No, no. Oh no. Don't worry. Everyone's OK. It's just me. I...

　　　　*(In another space, another world, **CLAIRE**, **GREG** and **ANTON** enter.)*

　　　　*(**GREG** walks with a limp.)*

ANTON. Did you hear?

CLAIRE. Hear what?

> (**GREG** *and* **ANTON** *look at each other uneasily.*)

ALLISON. You can watch us?

TAYLOR. Them.

ALLISON. You can watch what happens?

MARY. Sometimes. It's not always the best idea. It comes and goes.

GREG. We have something to tell you but you aren't going to like it so if this isn't the /time to tell you then we can –

CLAIRE. What. No. What. Oh no.

ALLISON. Claire isn't going to take it well. She had a very hard time. Everyone did. But Claire really did.

GREG. Do you want to go to the bathroom?

CLAIRE. No.

GREG. Let's sit /somewhere.

CLAIRE. No, tell me now.

ALLISON. Oh god.

TAYLOR. You can tell us what happened.

ALLISON. I just felt so bad you know? I kept hearing it. I kept thinking I would see *(To* **WILL**.*)* you, or... *(To* **MARY**.*)* you, or...

I felt bad that it wasn't me. And no one wants to talk about it. Everyone keeps saying, "You're young, live your life, it'll be OK," but I'm not young anymore. And I was living my life. I didn't know it but I was, I was doing things, and *after* I wasn't living my life, like, I can't live my life *now,* you stupid people. You can't live your life once you suddenly realize that you have a life and that it can be taken away from you. You can't forget something that happens to you, you're not the same after it happens to you, you aren't *you* anymore.

And it felt like no one wanted to talk about it. In any real way. People kept asking how I felt and...as if there is a word for it? As if I would know what that word is?

TAYLOR. Yeah, I know.

ALLISON. Mary, I thought you were mad at me.

MARY. What?

ALLISON. Like one day in rehearsal you kind of didn't talk to me and then it just seemed like it never got OK again and I don't know what I did but then you were gone, and I'm sorry. I don't know why you were mad. I really missed /you.

MARY. I missed you too, it was my fault, I missed you so much. It was me. I just. I thought it would be less hard to be me if I didn't talk to you. Because I wanted to be you. And I knew that I never could be.

ALLISON. Are you kidding, /you were the smartest, you were the best actor.

MARY. No, please, it doesn't matter what I was, I wanted to be you. But really I just wanted to not be me. I thought that I wouldn't be so hurt if I was someone else.

ALLISON. The hurt is so bad that it feels you can't live through it, right? And it never gets better, and everyone forgets, but inside you're screaming like "everything is wrong." And you go to guidance and –

TAYLOR. Did you see the bird lady?

ALLISON. Yeah. And she's nice, she tries but. Like you go in a room, still, and you look for the exit. Like doors slamming scare me.

EMILY. They all say that. When we watch.

ALLISON. And like seeing someone's parents? And they're so nice. They're just so nice, like we're little kids or something? And then feeling bad that they saw you because it makes them remember and it makes them upset, so just feeling bad that you exist?

CLAIRE. How did she do it?

GREG. Do you really want to know?

> (**CLAIRE** *looks at them, lost.*)

ANTON. Why don't we go sit somewhere –

CLAIRE. I don't want to be here anymore. I want to go.

GREG. Let's go.

CLAIRE. I want to go…somewhere where there's water.

ANTON. The lake.

CLAIRE. I want to go to the lake. But. Where's Sabreena? I need /Sabreena.

ANTON.	**GREG**.
I'll get her.	We'll find her.

> (*They head out.*)

> (**ALLISON** *sees* **BECKY**.)

ALLISON. Becky?

BECKY. Hi Allison.

ALLISON. Whoa, we haven't spoken to each other since the play.

BECKY. I know. It's a big school.

ALLISON. Yeah. Not that big.

BECKY. Yeah. But big enough that like we don't know each other.

ALLISON. We know each other.

BECKY. We do?

ALLISON. Of course we do. We did the play together. Your name is Becky.

BECKY. Your name is Allison.

ALLISON. My name is actually Iris. Allison is my middle name.

BECKY. Huh.

ALLISON. Yeah no one knows. I just hate Iris. It was my grandmother but I didn't know her and it makes me think about touching my eye.

BECKY. It's also a flower.

ALLISON. Don't tell anyone.

(**BECKY** *zips her lips.*)

BECKY. You are, like. Here, right?

ALLISON. Mm-hm. I am. And you're...?

BECKY. I'm just visiting. I just. Wanted to see everybody. It's not the same. Coming back isn't –

ALLISON. I know. But it's cool you can do that.

BECKY. It kind of feels like a big responsibility.

ALLISON. Well that's what it is to be the Stage Manager, right? It's a lot.

BECKY. It's a lot. I feel you on everything you said. Noises. How people look at you. God that's how we all looked at Cookie, wasn't it? And now everyone looks at all of us like that, and it's –

ALLISON. Sucks. It's so annoying.

BECKY. And. I feel like I have to do something. Something amazing. To like make up for it, to like...have it be worth it, have me be worth it.

ALLISON. You don't.

BECKY. I know, but /I feel like I do.

ALLISON. But I bet you *do* do something amazing. You do, don't you?

> *(And it's as if **BECKY** knows these things for the first time, and knows that they're true.)*

BECKY. I go to Penn.

ALLISON.	**EMILY**.
Oh. That's great, congratulations!	Really? That's so cool.

BECKY. Thanks.

MARY. To do –

BECKY. Finance. Well. Like business. But I want to do finance. I do finance.

ALLISON. You do?

BECKY. Yeah. I actually… I do really well. I do my undergrad there and then I go to Harvard.

EMILY.	**TAYLOR**.
You do??	Whooo!

EMILY. I want to go to Harvard! I mean…that's so awesome, I'm so happy for you!

BECKY. Yeah. In the future.

ALLISON.	**WILL**.
I'm not surprised. I knew you were smart.	Good for you.

BECKY. Thanks. And I uh get married. I have a little boy. When I'm thirty-three. I get married when I'm twenty-nine. I have Timothy at thirty-three.

ALLISON.	**MARY**.
Timothy! That's crazy.	Oh, yay.

BECKY. It's weird. It's not weird, actually, when it happens it just feels like the right thing to happen? Actually everything with Richard, that's the – yeah, everything with Richard just feels like the next thing was the right thing. So. It's good. We meet at Harvard.

ALLISON. Wow.

    (Beat.)

BECKY. I'm sorry, /Allison.

ALLISON. That's OK don't worry /about it.

BECKY. I um. I wish I had known that you were having a hard time.

ALLISON. Everyone's having a hard time, /you couldn't like –

BECKY. I know, but. Um. If you had wanted to talk, we could have.

ALLISON. Could we have?

    (They both wonder if it would have been possible.)

BECKY. We could have been like secret friends.

ALLISON. Ha yeah.

BECKY. Text or something. Email. Iris.

ALLISON. Shut up. That would have been nice.

    (They smile a little at each other.)

BECKY. Um. You know how like in the play. Emily /wanted to –

ALLISON. Yeah, no. Yeah, no. No, I don't want to go back.

BECKY. OK. Good.

ALLISON. I left. I know you can't go back. But could we. Could you show us some of your life, Becky? Like what you were talking about?

EMILY. Oh yes.

BECKY. Uh, I don't know.

ALLISON. Please?

WILL.	**EMILY**.
I would love /to see it.	Please, mrowr?

TAYLOR. Me too.

BECKY. I don't know how.

TAYLOR. You're the Stage Manager. You can make anything happen. And everyone will listen to you.

ALLISON. Mary is an amazing actress. Right Will?

WILL. Mary's the best. She can play anything.

BECKY. Well, I mean, if you're all OK with it, I guess we can try.

EMILY. Oh my god, it's like a play! It's like a play!!!!

> (**MARY** and **WILL** move their chairs to the middle of the stage.)

BECKY. But we don't do anything. Me and Richard. We sit at home and watch TV.

ALLISON. That's OK.

BECKY. We're parents.

WILL. Mary and I are professionals at playing parents.

BECKY. Like I have a really boring, normal /life.

TAYLOR. I'm a professional at being boring.

ALLISON. Just show us that. Your normal life would be just perfect, that would be really exciting. I love TV.

BECKY. OK. We have a couch. Our TV is here. We – we're really tired a lot of the time, especially after Timothy, so when he goes to bed we normally eat on the couch and watch TV at the end of the day.

(*They arrange this.*)

It's like /not exciting. It's like...being thirty-five.

TAYLOR.	**ALLISON.**
No, I love it.	This is perfect.

EMILY. It's a play!

ALLISON. OK, OK. Becky and Richard on the couch in the future. /You're married.

TAYLOR. Hold on, hold on, I do the narration and explainy bits around here. Ahem.

Welcome to...where do you live?

BECKY. Boston.[*]

TAYLOR.	**ALLISON.**	**WILL.**	**MARY.**	**EMILY.**
Woo, look at you!	Boston!	Ah, the Bruins!	Boston??	Ahhhh!

TAYLOR. OK, shhh, shh, shh. Good evening. This play is called *Becky's Life*. Welcome to Boston. Nice town, y'know what I mean? Becky and Richard are on the couch. It's the future. They have a kid, Timothy. They've just put him to bed.

(**EMILY** *makes a baby cry.*)

To bed.

EMILY. Oh.

---

[*] You can change this and subsequent references to any city that is aspirational to your students.

(**EMILY** *makes snoring noises.*)

TAYLOR. It's fall. It's the perfect part of fall, where the leaves are falling, and they shimmer, almost? Little yellow leaf tornados around you. The sky was bright blue all day. Now the sun's gone down. Earlier and earlier every day. It's cold outside, winter is telling you that it's coming, but inside their apartment Becky and Richard, and Timothy –

(**EMILY** *makes a laughing baby sound.*)

– are nice and warm. It's a Thursday night. They're thirty-five.

(**WILL** *and* **MARY** *look at each other. They kind of giggle.*)

(*They try to do this.*)

WILL AS RICHARD. How was work?

MARY AS BECKY. Uh. Good. Really good. I finished up this case,

(*She looks at* **BECKY**, *like, "do I have cases?" and* **BECKY** *nods.*)

and the lady I had been working with sent me an email that said she really liked working with me, and that I did a good job.

WILL AS RICHARD. Of course /she did.

MARY AS BECKY. No, but, well, I don't know.

WILL AS RICHARD. That's good.

MARY AS BECKY. Yeah, I felt really proud. It's like, *ugh*, for her to tell me?! Sometimes people don't tell you! She told me!

WILL AS RICHARD. She told you, yeah!

TAYLOR. There are all kinds of marriages. This is one of the good ones.

MARY AS BECKY. What do you want to eat tonight?

WILL AS RICHARD. Do you know what I want?

(**MARY AS BECKY** *laughs.*)

What?

MARY AS BECKY. That was so serious.

WILL AS RICHARD. Well, you /asked.

MARY AS BECKY. I know but now I feel I should prepare.

WILL AS RICHARD. I know exactly what I want and it's so rare that I do, I want a quarter-roasted chicken meal from that place that we ordered from like a /month ago.

MARY AS BECKY. Oh yeah!

WILL AS RICHARD. *(Continued.)* And French fries and onion rings and a piece of coconut cream pie for dessert.

MARY AS BECKY. Whoa.

WILL AS RICHARD. Oh my god, I want it so badly.

MARY AS BECKY. OK!

WILL AS RICHARD. Is that OK?

MARY AS BECKY. Yeah, that sounds /amazing!

WILL AS RICHARD. I want so much food. Isn't it crazy how we can just go get that? Like that something like that exists and that we can just go and we can have it? It's so nuts that you can want things and then you can do them.

MARY AS BECKY. Not all of them.

WILL AS RICHARD. Not all of them, but quarter chicken. Appetizer. Mozzarella sticks. That we can do.

MARY AS BECKY. That we can do.

WILL AS RICHARD. What are the things you want to do?

MARY AS BECKY. I dunno. Make pancakes this weekend. With a recipe that uses sour cream.

WILL AS RICHARD. *(Unsure.)* Mm.

MARY AS BECKY. No, the picture looked so good. And. Go through the car wash. Find a new song. And then listen to that song like a million times until I hate it. Sleep in a bed with fresh sheets. Hold a little puppy. That's so dorky. "Hold a little puppy," but they're so cute with the little face? Um. I would really like to go to Hungary, actually. I saw it on *Amazing Race* when I was watching with my mom like a million years ago but it looked nice, and no one every talks about it, so. Other places too, but I think that would be so cool. Go to the ocean. Watch Timothy in a school play. Make him a costume for it. See you. Talk to you. Hear about the things you are thinking. That's what I want to do, really. Be where you are. Forever.

WILL AS RICHARD. Well, good. 'Cause. That's what you got.

> *(**MARY** laughs. **BECKY** laughs. **ALLISON** and **TAYLOR** laugh.)*

MARY AS BECKY. That's good. That's all that I want. That's what I really want.

> *(The scene ends; **MARY** and **WILL** dissolve out of the space they were in.)*

TAYLOR. Was that right, Becky?

BECKY. That was perfect. That's way better than what actually happens, but. Well actually I don't know. I guess that really maybe is what it's like.

MARY. It's really good.

EMILY. It's as good as it's supposed to be.

BECKY. ...Yeah.

TAYLOR. Don't feel bad that you get it, Becky. Seriously.

MARY.	**EMILY.**
Yeah. I'm not jealous anymore.	Yeah.

TAYLOR. And it doesn't do us any good for you to feel bad.

> *(On earth, we see the lake.)*

> *(It's a beautiful day.)*

> *(If you are from a place with winter, it's like the first warm spring day that you've been trying to get to after months of darkness.)*

> *(It's that good. It's that beautiful.)*

Where are they?

EMILY.	**WILL.**
The lake.	The world.

> *(**SAM** and **REID** enter holding hands.)*

> *(**GREG, CLAIRE, ANTON, SABREENA, DJ,** and **COOKIE** are there.)*

> *(People have wet hair.)*

> *(The dead look at the living.)*

> *(The living are very very deep in grief.)*

> *(But they're at the lake.)*

> *(People swim. People take off their shoes.)*

> *(It is such a beautiful day.)*

ALLISON. It's so interesting just to watch people be people. Why didn't I realize that? It's so interesting how people do things.

MARY. It becomes kind of painful to watch.

EMILY. I think Sam's going to be famous. I think they're gonna do something really cool. Like win an Oscar for costume design, or like be Anna Wintour. But nice.

TAYLOR. I think that too. I've always thought that.

EMILY. Claire has this huge beautiful family.

MARY. Really?

EMILY. Yeah. They have a trailer and they all like go camping together. And she's a doctor.

MARY. Of course she is.

WILL. Anton's gonna invent a game that everyone plays.

TAYLOR. And DJ's gonna be his lawyer.

MARY. …And his dealer.

> *(They kind of laugh.* **ALLISON** *looks at* **BECKY**.*)*
>
> *(They talk to each other while the others continue.)*

ALLISON. It's really crazy that we did that play.

BECKY. I know.

TAYLOR. Reid's gonna be a teacher. All his students think he's so cool.

MARY. And he like "gets" the troubled ones.

TAYLOR.	**EMILY**.
Exactly.	Aw "troubled teens!"

ALLISON. It's so old...and we all have to play people who are so much older than ourselves. But also like. It's so much work. You did a lot of work.

BECKY. So did you.

TAYLOR. Greg's gonna be famous, too.

ALLISON. Yeah. But you really did.

TAYLOR. But like in an underground /way.

EMILY. He'll be in an Instagram scandal with a makeup person who sells bad primer.

TAYLOR. Yeah! And he'll make an apology video but /he'll be like, "Screw you, Nancy Drew!"

EMILY. He won't really apologize, that's it, that's totally it.

ALLISON. Like. You were in charge. You had to put all that stuff together.

BECKY. It wasn't a big /deal.

ALLISON. No but it was.

WILL. I hope Cookie keeps playing hockey.

TAYLOR. He does, he definitely does.

ALLISON. Because it's only because of all that stuff, right, like...

WILL. He's actually really good.

EMILY. Sabreena's going to have so many friends. She doesn't even know. But whenever she comes in the room, it's like all the windows open.

ALLISON. We all had to be told to come to rehearsal, we all had to do the work, the, the practicing again and again and that's why it was good. It was all those little things. And that was you. Thank you for doing all of that.

BECKY. You're welcome.

ALLISON. I had a really good time doing that play. Did you?

BECKY. *(Realizing.)* Yeah I did.

ALLISON. Do you remember when /Reid thought the horse was real?

BECKY. I know what you're gonna say – YES! Yes. And Sabreena like –

ALLISON. – had a FIT –

BECKY. Oh my god and was like *laughing*.

> *(They laugh remembering it.)*

Of course I remember that, that was like one of the best moments of my life.

> *(She realizes this is true.)*

ALLISON. It's nice to talk to you, Becky. I knew you'd be successful. I just knew it.

> *(**ALLISON** takes a seat among the dead.)*

> *(**BECKY** looks at them. She looks at **REID** and **SAM** and **DJ** and the others in the present at the lake.)*

> *(The lake somehow becomes a theatrical lake...like it's devolving from reality into an exercise you do in drama class.)*

> *(Maybe that's all it ever was?)*

> *(Everyone except **BECKY** starts to disappear.)*

> *(She turns to the audience.)*

BECKY. Uh. Thank you for coming.

I just, uh. I wanted to, uh. I needed...

I don't know. But. I felt I had to. I had to.

    (She crosses something off on her clipboard.)

So thank you for being here for it.

    (She looks up.)

I feel like there's something more I want to say. I don't know.

    (She looks at individual people in the audience.)

I guess I hope you all have really happy lives?

Thank you for coming. Thank you for being here.

Thanks.

Goodbye.

    (She goes.)

End of Play

www.ingramcontent.com/pod-product-compliance
Lightning Source LLC
Chambersburg PA
CBHW070633120726
47909CB00004B/1414